THE

LIGHT

BOOK ONE OF THE LIGHT SERIES

JACQUELINE BROWN

Cover art by Aero Gallerie.

Also by Jacqueline Brown:
Through the Ashes, Book Two of The Light Series
From the Shadows, Book Three of The Light Series
Before the Silence, A Light Series Short Story

To download your FREE copy of *Before the Silence* please
visit www.Jacqueline-Brown.com

This book is dedicated to the man of my dreams, Daniel.
It is an honor to be your wife.
Thank you for sharing your life with me.

One

I glanced at the rearview mirror: a wall of darkness followed us. My gaze moved to the clock on the dash. The small red numbers read twelve twenty-nine. I hadn't seen another car for almost half an hour.

Josh sat behind me, his arm around Blaise. Her black hair against his white, long-sleeved T-shirt made a striking contrast. They wrapped up in a blanket and were asleep within minutes after our last stop. They'd barely moved in the last hundred miles or so.

Sara sat in the passenger seat beside me. She was quiet for the moment, looking down at her phone. She'd been talking or texting almost nonstop since we left the city. She'd never been good with silence.

She put her phone in her lap and looked up at me. "How long until we stop, Bria?"

"You know patience is a virtue," I answered, turning to glance in her direction, her curly black hair almost disappearing against the dark window.

"Yeah, yeah, I know. And you're as bad at it as I am."

She twisted toward me in her seat.

"You've got a point," I said. "I can go another three hundred miles or so before I need gas."

Sara lifted her head and then dropped it again in her usual dramatic style. "Ugh, that is so long. Let's stop and get a coffee."

"Sara, look out your window. What do you see?"

She turned her head. "Trees."

"Let me know when you see a coffee shop, and I'll stop," I said as I watched the trees become illuminated and then disappear into the darkness.

"Just stop at the next gas station. Any coffee is better than no coffee." She clicked her phone on and then off again.

"I'll stop as soon as I see something," I said. "I could use a break, anyway."

"Thanks," she said, looking out the window.

Her phone went from dark to bright every other second or so. When it lit up, the night outside became darker and harder to see. It was irritating, but I didn't say anything. This trip was for her, to help her get over her newest broken heart … but I knew it was also about me.

The trees seemed to be getting denser. The highway was narrow and the woods vast. I used to spend time among trees. But these memories were fuzzy. My mom had loved being outside. It seemed that when she died, my time in nature died too. My father moved us from North Carolina up to DC, and I hadn't been in the woods since. I brushed a tear from my eye. Eighteen years later and it still hurt every time I thought of her. I tried hard never to think of her.

"You okay?" Sara asked.

I hadn't noticed she was watching me.

I wiped my eyes with the back of my left hand. "Yeah, I guess I'm more tired than I thought," I answered.

Sara and I had been friends for a long time. She knew me well enough to know that when I cried it was because of my mom. She also knew I didn't want to talk about it.

She nodded, but continued to watch me from the corner of her eyes.

Putting her phone down, she asked, "Didn't you grow up near here?"

I looked at the GPS on my dash. "I don't remember. I know we lived in North Carolina, but that's all I know."

"Do you remember the address? I could find it on my phone." She picked up her phone, clicking it on.

"Why?" I asked.

"I don't know. If we're going to be near it, we could take a small detour and check it out." She placed her phone face down on her jeans. A pale light escaped from all sides of it.

"You know there's nothing left," I said, feeling the anger rise.

"Oh yeah, I forgot. Sorry," she said, twisting forward in her seat and looking away from me.

After a moment of silence, she said, "Are you getting tired? Do you want me to drive?"

"No, I'm fine," I said. At least, driving offered me some distraction. Sitting in a dark car with nothing to do, going down roads that reminded me of home—that would not be good.

"Okay. I didn't really want to, but I was trying to be nice," she said.

I knew her feelings were hurt. My tone had been harsher than I meant it to be. She went back to messing with her phone. I loved Sara, but she was always on her phone. She never had actual silence. There might not be noise, but there was never quiet. We were alike in that way. I wasn't as addicted to screens as she was, but I did what I could to avoid silence. In the silence my thoughts came—thoughts I didn't want to have.

I glanced in the mirror. Blaise and Josh were the opposite of Sara and me. They loved silence. When we were going out at night, they'd be going to sleep. They were content just being. Sara and I, if we were being honest, were never content.

The four of us made an unlikely group; still, we were the best of friends. I met Blaise and Sara my freshman year. Blaise and I were roommates. We hated each other for the first semester. Well, I hated her. She had said she just didn't like me. Sara and I had class together and were instantly drawn to each other. Blaise says we are too alike for our own good. Eventually Sara and Blaise became friends, and then I let go of my hatred and realized Blaise was amazing. A year later she met Josh. He was nothing like any guy Sara or I had ever dated. He was good to his core.

When he proposed, I was almost as excited as Blaise. The wedding is set for the day after we all graduate. They will be young newlyweds, only twenty-two. Normally I would make fun of someone getting married that young, or assume they were pregnant. But with Blaise and Josh it all made sense, and they couldn't be pregnant. They were both virgins.

Tears welled as I pushed down the choices of my past.

Headlights appeared behind us.

"Happy Thanksgiving, Bria," Sara said, turning her head toward me.

"Happy Thanks—"

In an instant the night sky became brighter than day. My right hand flew up to keep the light from piercing my eyes. I blinked, forcing my eyes open. A moment later complete darkness overtook the false daylight. Just as the light had been artificial, so too was the dark. My eyes hurt and I could see nothing.

"What's going on?" Sara's voice sounded shaken.

"I don't know." I realized the car was suddenly silent. The engine was no longer working. The brake pedal was hard to push and did almost nothing to slow us.

I breathed deeply, trying to control the panic threatening to overtake me. "I can't control the car," I said. I blinked again and again, trying to clear my eyes. Shadows started to appear. I exhaled. I wasn't blind.

"What?" she asked, her voice higher pitched than normal.

I stomped on the pedals, one after the other. Nothing happened.

"I can't do anything. The gas pedal, the brake, they aren't working." I heard the thump-thump-thump of the serrated edge of the road. I tried hard to pull us back into the lane. "The steering wheel isn't working. Help me!" I screamed, losing all ability to control my surging panic.

Sara put both hands on the steering wheel, and we both pulled as hard as we could to stay on the road.

"Thanks," I said, as we got centered on the highway.

"What's going on?" Blaise asked, her voice groggy and

scared.

Sara turned to face her. "There was a bright light, and the car stopped working," she said.

"What do you mean?" Josh said, his voice scratchy from sleep.

"Just what I said. There was a light, and now the car is dead." Sara reached for the phone in her lap.

"It's not working," she said, as if she couldn't believe her own words.

I heard Blaise and Josh digging to find their phones.

"Ours are dead too," Blaise said with the same unbelief Sara had.

I picked mine up as we rolled to a stop. I pushed the button … nothing happened. I tried again and again. "Nothing," I said, putting it back in the cup holder.

Blaise whispered, "What are we going to do?"

We sat staring at each other, at the night. No one spoke. My heart raced as I realized I had no idea what to do. None of us had any idea what to do. The car, our phones, tablets, even our watches were all dead. We were in the middle of Nowhere, North Carolina, completely stranded … six hundred miles from home, with no way to get help.

Sara's words broke the silence: "We are going to die."

Two

I summoned the strength to get out of the car. The cold seeped through my thin tunic and leggings in an instant. The knee-high boots offered some warmth, though no comfort, thanks to the one-and-a-half-inch heels. I shivered and wrapped my arms around my body. I hadn't brought warm clothes; none of us had. The forecast for Palm Beach had been in the upper eighties. I'd packed three bikinis and no winter coat.

Blaise was still wrapped in the blanket she and Josh had been sleeping under. Sara and I joined her. We huddled together as we stared at the car. Josh had an arm around Blaise's shoulders.

Without the beams of headlights, I could see the light of the moon clearly. How long had it been since I noticed moonlight? There was enough light for me to see the barren silver trees that surrounded us.

Looking at my friends, I saw the same fear and confusion they saw on my face. I thought of Sara's words and wondered if she was right.

I turned toward the north, the direction the light had come from. I detected movement.

"There are people walking toward us," I whispered, trying hard to stay calm.

Sara and I moved closer to each other. Josh stepped in front of us. Blaise dropped her end of the blanket and stood next to him. He edged himself in front of her, his body tense.

"Come on," Sara whispered. We walked forward and stood next to our friends, the blanket still wrapped around us.

As the figures neared I could see that they were about our age. He was older and she was younger, but neither looked older than twenty-five. He carried a duffel bag. She wore a backpack and dragged a small rolling suitcase behind her. He was about Josh's height, maybe a little taller, six foot two or so. She was also tall, probably five nine. As they neared, he opened his hands toward us in the universal "I come in peace" gesture.

Sara whispered in my ear, "He's cute, really cute."

"Shh," I hissed back. But she was right. He was way above average on the cuteness scale, and, for that matter, so was the woman with him. They made a cute couple. He looked a few years older than her, though not many. Beneath the purple dye I could tell her hair was blonde. His was light brown. Unlike Sara and me, they were dressed for warmth and comfort. Neither wore something you could buy in a department store or boutique. Perhaps a camping store, but I had never been in one to know for sure.

"I'm Jonah and this is East," he said, stopping a few feet from Josh.

Josh introduced each of us. It was funny to watch the interaction. Josh wasn't the tough sort of guy. He was the sweet, lovable "call for Blaise when there was a big spider" kind of guy. But tonight he seemed to be channeling his testosterone-laden ancestors. He was ready to protect us. I loved him for that. I could tell Blaise did too. She was staying calm, trying to be as threatening as her yoga-teaching self could be. Yet, I could see her glance at Josh with a new appreciation.

"Where were you headed?" East asked, her voice calm.

"Palm Beach," Blaise responded, her tone matching East's. Blaise grabbed Josh's hand, and his body visibly relaxed.

Jonah matched the relaxed posture.

"What about you?" Blaise asked, her voice getting back to its normal calm tone.

"Home," Jonah responded, looking at Blaise as he spoke.

"Where's that?" I asked, pulling the blanket tighter

around me while eyeing Blaise's heavy winter coat, jeans, and sneakers with envy.

"The next exit and then about twenty miles east," Jonah answered. The way he looked at me caused me to shiver, or maybe it was the cold.

"I'm sorry, but you look familiar," he said, realizing he'd been staring at me.

"Do I? I don't think I have ever seen you before," I answered, knowing there was no way I had. He was someone I would not forget.

"No, I guess not," he said, still looking puzzled.

Sara pulled the blanket tighter around her body, our hands meeting between us as we attempted to stay warm. She said, "Do you know what happened? We saw a light, and then everything stopped working."

"My brother thinks he knows," East said, nodding her head toward Jonah.

Sara said nothing, but I knew she was jumping up and down on the inside, realizing they weren't a couple.

Josh looked at Jonah. "What do you think it was?"

I relaxed as Jonah's gaze shifted from me to Josh. "An EMP," he said.

"A what?" Sara asked in her "stupid girl" voice, the one she used when she was into a guy. I rolled my eyes before I could stop myself. How she could go from thinking we were going to die, to being totally focused on a cute stranger in five minutes was beyond me.

Jonah answered, "Electromagnetic pulse. I think that's what this must have been. It disables everything electronic."

"I've heard of those," Blaise said, "but this couldn't have been one."

"Why not?" Jonah said, setting his duffel bag on the ground.

"There's no way there could be one that huge. For it to knock out all of our things, that would mean—" Blaise stopped. She pulled in closer to Josh.

"A nuclear reaction," Jonah said, finishing her thought.

She nodded, holding Josh's hand tighter. He put his arm around her.

"Here? In the U.S.?" Sara asked, her voice back to normal.

I knew that the idea of a nuclear explosion in the U.S. was an impossibility to all of us.

Jonah nodded. "Not necessarily on the ground, but in the atmosphere above us," he said.

"How?" I asked. "How could that happen?" I stared at him in disbelief.

"Not by accident," East said, anger in her eyes.

"An … attack?" Blaise said, almost unable to say the words.

"It's the only thing that makes sense," Jonah said.

Josh looked up to the sky. "But it doesn't make sense. We aren't at war with anyone," he said.

"We're always fighting someone," East said. "Even if our government doesn't call it a war. And since when do terrorists need a war to attack us," she said, her voice harsh and cynical.

She was right. We all knew the possibility of an attack was real. But one that knocked out our phones and cars? That seemed impossible, no matter how probable these strangers thought it was.

"So what do we do? Wait for someone to find us?" I asked, tired of the silence and the cold.

Jonah looked at me, his expression confused. "Wait?" he asked.

"For someone to give us a ride," I said, confused by his confusion.

"Who do you think is coming for us? Who do you think can?" He sounded frustrated and sad at the same time.

"Eventually someone is going to drive by," I said, irritation in my voice. "I mean, it's the middle of the night in the middle of nowhere, so it might take a while. Plus, if some cars on the road got zapped by whatever this was, then it will take longer. But tomorrow is Thanksgiving. Someone is going to drive by soon."

Jonah exhaled and looked at me. "If you had a weapon big enough to knock out all things electronic, where would you set it off? In the country, where there aren't many people, or in the cities, where there are millions? I don't think we haven't seen anyone because no one decided to drive down the interstate. I think we haven't seen anyone because everyone else's cars are as dead as ours. And the fact that we haven't seen anyone come from the south tells me the range was either really far or there was more than one," he said.

My knees buckled. I leaned on Sara. My mind raced— the thoughts were fleeting and made no sense. I saw images of cities with no lights, no power. Places with unchanged structures whose inhabitants had lost all sense of what the world was. I thought of my dad and wished I was with him.

"You all can come with us," Jonah's words were tense, but I could sense the kindness beneath his tone. "Get what you can from your car."

"Thank you. That's very nice of you," Blaise said, her voice somber.

She was the calm one of our group. She neither minimized nor exaggerated experiences. She took them as they were presented to her, with as little judgment as possible. She often said things weren't good or bad, they just were. I wondered now what she thought of all that was happening around us.

Sara looked from East to Jonah, her eyes pleading. "What about our families?" she asked.

"Where are you all from?" East's tone was softer and less cynical.

"We go to school at Columbia," Blaise said, "but our families are all over. My parents are in Pennsylvania and Josh's parents and sisters are in Nebraska."

"My mom and sister live near DC," Sara said, looking down as she spoke.

I knew I was supposed to say something, but I couldn't. The lump in my throat grew as I realized that if Jonah and East were right, if this was an attack, then our nation's capital would've been a primary target in this attack, and my father with it. How would it defend itself now, without machines or electronics of any kind? Even if the city had survived invaders, the chaos brought on by the food and water shortages would cut it to its knees. The place I was raised. The place my father still lived would be destroyed and my father with it.

Blaise spoke for me. "Bria's dad is in DC too."

Sara lifted her head and looked at me. "We can't just leave them," she said, her voice shaking.

"What can we do?" I asked, barely loud enough for my own ears to hear.

"We have to try," she replied in a pleading tone. "We can't leave them in DC. It was probably the target."

I knew Sara was right. But I also knew there was nothing we could do.

East stepped toward us. "For now you should come with us. You can figure out what to do when we know more," she said.

Sara stiffened. "No, we can't abandon our families," she said. "*I* can't abandon *my* family." Tears were running down her face.

"Sara, we don't have food or water. Or any way to stay warm," Blaise said, putting her hand on Sara's shoulder.

"We wouldn't make it," I said, looking at her, my voice stronger.

"We have to try," Sara said again.

"We would die. There's no way we wouldn't," I said, my voice firm.

Josh stepped toward us. "I think we should go with East and Jonah. From there we can think it through more, and prepare," he said, his voice emotional yet steady.

Sara said nothing. I took her hand. She pulled it away.

Josh held tightly to Blaise's hand. They were to become each other's family in a year, but now, with their parents so far away, it seemed they had just become the only family they had. Sara and I were alone.

* * *

On my back I carried my school bag, emptied of books, now full of clothes from my large suitcase. I balanced my purse on the small roller bag I dragged down the interstate. Both had been emptied of much of their prior contents, and now contained the necessities, as Blaise and Josh had insisted on. I had pulled on the only pair of jeans I had, over the thin leggings. I traded my heeled boots for running shoes, and found a forgotten running jacket stuffed in the back of my trunk. Everyone else had a coat. It had been freezing when we left New York, but I refused to take mine partly because I was in an obstinate mood and partly because I was already thinking of the warm Florida Thanksgiving we were going to bask in.

It was supposed to be a relaxing trip. We were taking Sara away to help her forget about her latest short-lived relationship, but I knew it was also to get me away from Trent. None of my friends liked him, and I couldn't blame them.

As for Trent, he believed he was a catch. And on the outside he was. He was rich, handsome, well-connected, well-educated, driven, and intelligent. But on the inside he was mean, self-absorbed, judgmental, and borderline abusive. Some stay in unhealthy relationships because they don't see the unhealth. I stayed because I did and knew I deserved it.

Trent had asked me to go skiing with him for Thanksgiving. Sara made a plea that she needed to get away and wanted to go to Florida. Blaise and Josh agreed a trip to Florida would be just the thing to help Sara. Trent tried to get me to choose him over my friends. It turned into a fight, and in the end he decided to go with some friends to Las Vegas because he knew it would hurt me. He knew I detested the friends he was going with. I knew exactly what they were going to do when they were in "sin city" and I hated them for it. I felt anger rise and burn my cheeks. I deserve very little because I bring very little. I know this, and Trent reminded me often. Even so, I believe in monogamy and that much I did bring and did deserve.

I took a deep breath. How much of that mattered now? Trent had probably landed an hour before the light flashed. Had there been a light on the West Coast as well? If so, Las Vegas would've been hit. How would Trent survive in the desert, in the winter, where food and water basically have to be bussed in? How would anyone?

I reached for my phone in my back pocket; I wanted to call him to see if he was okay. As my hand touched it, I remembered what I had forgotten. It didn't work, nothing worked. As stupid as it was, I couldn't bring myself to leave my phone behind. None of us could. Though none of us said it, I knew we each hoped that somehow they would work again. That somehow we were overestimating the seriousness of the situation and our phones could be fixed. The pit in my stomach told me that, if anything, we were underestimating the seriousness of the situation.

I turned to look at my car. It had been swallowed by the darkness.

Three

I could see the faint hint of the rising sun as we trudged past the exit sign that read HOODVILLE. A strange feeling came over me as I read the word, but a moment later it passed. My gaze shifted to Jonah, walking a few paces ahead of me. The muscles of his left arm bulged from the weight of the duffel bag he carried. I don't know if I could have carried it for more than a few feet; he made it look effortless.

He and East set the pace. Sara, Blaise, and I walked side by side and Josh brought up the rear. It was clear that East and Jonah were in the best shape, but they were also motivated to get home. The rest of us had nothing that we were walking toward, and with each step south we got farther from our families. We had no other option. Not today, anyway.

Thinking of my friends, I worried we might not be accepted as readily as we would've been yesterday. My skin was pale and my hair was light, like Jonah's and East's and probably most of the people who lived in this part of the state, but my friends were various shades of tan and brown. Blaise had been adopted from China when she was a baby. Her skin was as light as mine, but her eyes were blacker than her jet-black hair. Sara called herself a melting pot. Her grandparents all hailed from different parts of the world— Germany, Ireland, Africa, Brazil. The result was my exquisitely beautiful friend. Her skin was light brown, her curly hair black, and her eyes like emeralds too dark for light to pierce. Out of the four of us, Josh was the darkest. His mother was from Guatemala and his dad from Nebraska. He looked as though he could be from the Middle East. It made me nervous for him.

If we assumed, like Jonah did, that we had been attacked, then the obvious question was who attacked us? The relationship between the United States and China had become increasingly hostile. All trade had been stopped between the nations two months ago. Prices of everything had soared. Blaise had already started to deal with hate-filled people on the street. Then, of course, there was the constant tension in the Middle East.

None of my friends were oblivious to how their appearance shaped their interactions with people … especially in recent years as global conflicts increased. For the most part they never had any trouble, but whatever this was, just changed the world. Jonah and East didn't seem to care, but what about their family? What about the people who lived in this rural part of North Carolina?

Jonah and East led the way off the interstate. The exit was so small and the area so rural that there wasn't anything more than a stop sign on either side of the interstate.

We walked off the interstate, facing the sliver of sun that was beginning to mark the start of a new day—one that was categorically different than yesterday, when I had woken up in the apartment I shared with Blaise and Sara. My alarm clock played whatever song was on my playlist at the moment. I took a hot shower and ate scrambled eggs. Today there would be no songs on playlists, no hot showers or hot meals. No electricity of any kind, if Jonah was right. I feared he was.

I thought of my father. How would he survive without power or transportation? How would he get food? How would any of them? How would we?

With food on my mind, I couldn't move past it. I was suddenly aware of a growing hunger and an almost overpowering thirst.

"Can we stop?" I asked, not caring what the response was. I stopped dragging the suitcase to fish through my purse for the half a bottle of water and protein bar. The suitcase fell flat. I cared for half a second and then realized I was too tired to care about anything. I sat on top of it. My feet throbbed as I removed the weight of my body from them. I was in decent shape, but walking for five hours up and down the rolling hills of North Carolina, dragging a suitcase, not having slept for twenty-four hours, it was all taking its toll. I wanted to cry, but refused. Not because I was being tough; I knew once I started I wouldn't be able to stop.

"I recommend you sip your water and eat as little food as you need to," Jonah announced to the group, though he was looking at me.

He and East stopped a few feet ahead of the rest of us, each of them reaching for their metal water bottle and then sitting on the ground.

"He's right. We don't know how long it will take us to find more of either," Josh added as he slipped Blaise's backpack from his back.

She sat and he followed. They were so in sync. They rarely needed to speak to one another; they seemed to read each other's mind. He took a small sip of his water bottle before passing it to her. She took an equally small sip and put it back in her backpack. Sara sat by my feet. I gave her half of my protein bar. We nibbled and sipped our waters.

Blaise looked at us. "I keep thinking this has to be a bad dream."

I could hear the exhaustion in her voice. Her straight

black hair, which was usually so neat, was in a messy ponytail. Josh put his arm around her and she sank into him. He wrapped his other arm around her and laid his head on hers as she cried silent tears. Sara reached out and rubbed her shin. Blaise held on tightly to Sara's hand.

I sat, trying not to feel. I didn't want to acknowledge the pain Blaise was feeling because that would mean I had to acknowledge my own pain, my own fear of this new world, and I didn't have the strength to do that.

"How far until we get to your house?" I asked, my voice cracking as I looked at East and Jonah.

"About twenty miles, so maybe six hours or so," Jonah answered.

He watched me in a way that made me uneasy. He didn't look at me in a creepy-guy way. I think I would have preferred that look. At least I understood it and knew to keep my guard up. The look he gave me made no sense. It was as if he was trying to figure something out. Figure me out, I suppose, but why would he care?

I was tired of sitting.

I stood and repositioned my backpack. He watched as I did so and then quickly turned away. As if he suddenly realized he was staring.

Everyone stood up silently. No one was ready to move,

though everyone understood we had to keep going.

We walked facing the sun. I dug through my purse and found my oversized sunglasses. Slipping them on made me feel a little more normal. Not everything was different. They also provided me with some privacy. My eyes could not be seen and neither could my tears.

The road we were on was small, two lanes. Trees bordered both sides. Yesterday I would have said it was pretty, with the last of the leaves floating to the ground in the early-morning sun, and crunching softly beneath our feet as we walked. But today, "pretty" felt like a luxury. Survival was all that mattered now.

As we trudged on we came across a small black car with a yellow bumper sticker that read: I BELIEVE. I had no idea what that meant and I didn't care.

When Jonah and East saw it, they came to life.

"Eli made it, he made it home!" East shouted as she ran up and hugged the car.

"I thought he wasn't driving up until today. Thank God he came early," Jonah said, putting his arm around East.

"Thank you, God," she said as she lifted her gaze to the sky.

They hugged, not seeming to want to let go of one another.

"This is our older brother's car." East was practically laughing as she told us. "He said he couldn't get away until today, but this is his car, so he must have made it."

"He'll be home by now," Jonah said, looking at the dead watch on his wrist.

Blaise said, "That is wonderful. We'll all try and walk faster so you two can get home to your family."

She was always so kind. I knew she missed her parents, yet she was happy for East and Jonah.

Jonah and East picked up their forgotten luggage. "Thanks," they said in unison, and smiled at each other some more. Their joy was contagious.

As the leaves crunched underfoot and the rising sun started to warm the cold air, I realized that I was lucky. Even if I wasn't walking toward my home where my parents and sibling waited for me, I was still lucky. I had my family with me. I missed my father, though he left me long ago. I knew he loved me, but even as a child I realized he was afraid of love. He loved my mom, and he lost her. The loss was too much for him.

I can't remember him before her death, and I can barely remember my mom at all. What I can remember is the love I felt when I was with them. It was an overwhelming, all-encompassing love that I have never felt since. My parents had loved so deeply, and they had loved me so deeply. I wished desperately she had lived, that I had grown up with that love, but at least I had it even if for a short time. Others, like Sara, never knew it.

Her parents fought, physically fought throughout her childhood, before her mom finally escaped with her and her sister when Sara was ten. Her father eventually located them, but no longer physically beat her mom; instead, he fought her in court for custody of them. He had money; her mom did not—he made sure of that. He won. Sara and her sister only saw their mom every other weekend and a few weeks during school breaks. With their mom gone, his violence turned to his daughters. Sara said he never beat them like he had their mom, but he "punished" them when he thought they deserved it. She said that was often. She took "her share" of the abuse and her sister's too; she did what she could to protect her.

When her sister was thirteen and she was sixteen, the girls begged the judge to let them live with their mother. Despite their father's attorneys doing everything they could to discredit their mother, the judge agreed to let them go home. Once her dad could no longer hurt her mother by keeping them from her, he left. He moved out of state and stopped paying child support, causing Sara's mom to pick up a second job cleaning offices at night. Sara also worked to help support herself and her little sister. She worked hard in school and got a scholarship to Columbia. She hadn't seen her dad since she was seventeen. If she had her wish, she would never see him again.

At Columbia she started going to the counseling center. She knew she needed help. She soon understood that she sought out guys because she needed love, but even though she understood it, she still did it. She had more one-night stands than she wanted to remember. She felt horrible about herself and had on more than one occasion come back to our apartment, sobbing in the early-morning hours. But then she'd meet someone new and do it all again. It was her addiction. I knew by the way she looked at Jonah that he was her newest drug. I felt sorry for both of them.

I understood her behavior. I had done the same thing when I was younger. I was desperate for love and attention. Guys, the wrong guys, could sense my desperation and flocked to me. I made a lot of really stupid choices, but then I made one mistake that was unforgivable. After that, I stopped looking for love or attention. I realized I deserved neither.

Trent came along during my junior year of college. He was charming and incredibly persistent. Most guys moved on pretty quickly when I turned them down, but not Trent. Time after time he showed up with flowers, poems, homemade desserts. He was Prince Charming and he made me feel like a princess. That all changed after we started dating. And after we slept together, any remnant of Prince Charming was scrubbed away. I wanted to leave, but I kept thinking—and he kept telling me—it was my fault that he changed, and if I would be a better girlfriend he would get back to who he was before. I loved that person and I wanted him back, so I tried and tried. After a year of trying, I realized that this was who he was. The Prince Charming was only a facade, a ploy he used to lure me in. From then on I stopped trying, but I didn't leave.

Sara, probably because she grew up with domestic violence, saw through him first, and has hated him ever since. The three of them tried to protect me, tried to keep me from being alone with him. They were pretty effective. He only ever hit me once. Josh confronted Trent about the bruises and threatened to call the police if he ever did it again. Trent knew I wouldn't call the police. He also knew I wouldn't lie to the police; he didn't have that much power over me—not yet, anyway. So he begged for my forgiveness and swore he had changed. He said if I would be "good," then he would too.

For our one-year anniversary he took me to Cape Cod. It was the first time we had spent any real time alone since he hit me a few months before. I promised my friends it would be fine. Trent was on his best behavior as we drove and that first night, but when we woke up the next morning he was his old self. He didn't hit me, but he criticized everything I did—even the way I brushed my hair. I could see in his eyes that he wanted to control me, not love me.

When we came back I told my friends it had been a great long weekend, just what we needed. I don't know why I lied to them. I thought they believed me. But ever since, they had been sticking to me, not even letting me go to dinner with Trent without coming along. Sometimes they showed up where we were. Trent hated them; they kept him from having full control over me. He threatened me many times that he was going to leave if I didn't tell them to back off. He told me he just wanted to spend time alone with me, without them always being there. I talked to my friends about it, but they didn't care. They continued showing up or calling me or texting me constantly if I was with him.

The ski trip was an ultimatum. Either I went with him, or we were done. The truth was, I didn't want to go with him, but I never would have admitted that to anyone. When I told my friends about the invitation to go skiing, they concocted this scheme of getting me to Florida. I agreed pretty easily, saying I didn't like skiing. Now Trent and I were on opposite sides of the country, with no way to span the distance between Vegas and North Carolina.

No tears came.

I had been walking in silence for longer than I realized, not seeing what was in front of me. At some point the road had turned. The sun was now blocked by trees. I looked around. Sara walked silently beside me. I could only imagine the variety of thoughts running through her mind. She tried to avoid silence, saying she didn't like what it did to her. I wondered how she was handling this. Her expression was blank, as I'm sure mine had been moments before when I was lost in my own mind. East and Jonah led the way, and spoke now and then. When they did, it seemed to be about their family.

Behind me I heard Josh whispering to Blaise.

"It's just weird. There are no houses, no other cars besides their brother's, no stores, no nothing. I mean, we don't even know these people. We don't know that they didn't somehow create that light and disable our car and electronics and now they are leading us into the woods to do who knows what."

"You seriously think they would disable our car and electronics just to walk us through the woods for fourteen hours?" Blaise said. "There are easier ways to kidnap people, and ways that don't involve somehow keeping all other cars off the interstate and making yourself carry all of your belongings for hours on end. I don't think we are that enticing of a target."

I could tell Blaise was trying not to sound too irritated.

Josh lowered his voice even more. "The point is, we don't know them. They could be serial killers. I mean, she does have purple hair and tattoos. You never know about those people."

"Honey, you are really tired. You have a tattoo, and for Halloween I dyed my hair pink and it ended up looking purple," Blaise answered.

"Yeah, but my tattoo is small. Hers is like her whole forearm, and it's okay to dye hair on Halloween."

"Her tattoo is a cross," Blaise answered.

"No, it's a crucifix. It creeps me out. It's weird to see Jesus nailed to a cross on her arm."

"Josh, let it go. They are nice. I like her purple hair and her 'creepy' cross tattoo," Blaise spat back.

"Fine. But don't say I didn't warn you when we end up being dinner."

"Oh, honestly!"

She sped up and started walking with Sara and me.

"The conversation in the back was wearing me out. What are you two talking about?" she said.

I looked at her. "I think we have each been lost in thought," I said.

Sara wiped her eyes quickly. I pretended not to notice.

"Well then, what have you been thinking about?"

Blaise said, looking at me.

"Trent, I guess."

"Yeah? What about him?" Josh said as he sped up to walk with us.

Blaise shot a hard look at him. "Are you going to be reasonable? Because this conversation is for reasonable people only."

"Like you said, I'm tired. I get a little crazy when I'm tired."

"Yes, you do. You are forgiven," Blaise said, her face softening.

Josh gave her an "I'm sorry" look. "Now, what about Trent?" he said.

All eyes turned to me. It even seemed that Jonah and East stopped chatting to listen—though they didn't turn their heads or slow their pace.

"I'm pretty sure that me coming on this trip meant that we are through," I answered.

"Why do you say that?" Sara asked.

"He told me so," I said with a shrug.

Blaise looked at me. "He's threatened to break up with you a million times before. The key is not what he wants, it's what you want."

"That's just it," I answered. "I think the farther away from him I walk, the better I feel."

"Yes!" Josh tried to jump, but weighed down by

luggage, the result was a small hop. "I mean, that seems like a reasonable thought. Continue, please," he said after Blaise shot him a "Calm down and let her talk" look.

"It's almost like I can breathe better out here," I said.

"You probably can," Blaise responded. "The pollution is not near as bad as in New York."

"Yeah, but it's more than that. It's like things are clearer. Like some sort of fog is leaving my mind," I said.

"I know what you mean," Sara said. "Things are becoming clearer to me too."

Four

A dog barked in the distance. It was the first connection to other humans in the hours since we saw Eli's car.

East grabbed Jonah's arm in panic. "The electric fence won't be working," she said, her voice shaking.

At that moment a large black dog appeared out of nowhere. He charged, growling and snarling. Jonah lunged forward, getting in front of East. He clenched the duffel bag in front of him. It would be his weapon. The muscles in his arms and back were noticeable against the long-sleeved T-shirt he wore.

The dog stopped, his nose a foot from Jonah's hands. He stood, pawing the ground, muscles pulsing, hair raised, open mouth exposing fangs dripping with saliva. His head bigger than a human's, his shoulders broader than his head. He was terrifying and he stood ready to attack, but didn't.

"He must not know the fence is disabled," East whispered to Jonah. She grabbed onto his shirt and slowly pulled him back. She cautiously moved to retrieve her discarded luggage, never turning her back on the dog.

Jonah stepped backward, not turning his body, keeping his eyes on the dog at all times.

"Walk behind me. Don't turn your back to him," Jonah said, trying to calm his voice. But the tension was noticeable.

Sara, Josh, Blaise, East, and I walked backward to the opposite side of the road, angling east the entire time. Once we were across the road Jonah walked backward at a faster pace. The dog ran along the edge of where the electric fence had been, staying as close to us as he could. He barked and growled.

"Their property line ends soon," East whispered, her voice still shaky. "He'll think he has to stop."

We walked on and the dog followed as long as he could. At the corner his stance changed. He stopped, lifted his head as if listening to something, turned, and ran back in the direction he had come.

We all exhaled in unison.

"I hadn't realized I was holding my breath," I whispered to Sara.

"Me either," she said.

East was shaking as she walked quickly forward, the rest of us almost jogging to keep up with her.

"Do you know the people who live there?" Blaise asked.

East did not turn or slow her pace. Jonah answered, "Yes."

"Are they nice?" Sara asked.

"No," he said, the hatred evident in his voice.

East said nothing.

* * *

A dirt road divided the long, weathered, gray fence in half. A large iron gate stood connecting the two halves, making them one.

"We'll have to climb the fence. We won't be able to open the gate, without the key to unlock the electronic arms," Jonah said.

He angled off the road into the dry ditch that separated the fence from the road. His legs disappeared up to his thighs. He walked to the other side and threw his duffel bag over the fence. How effortless he made it all look. East walked down the ditch, dragging her suitcase behind her. She climbed over the fence. Jonah handed her the suitcase. Josh helped Blaise down and she slipped once. Jonah offered her his hand as she climbed out of the ditch and over the fence. Josh followed. Sara and I went next. Each of us dragged our luggage, stepping slowly down the ditch so we wouldn't slip on the dry, crunchy earth. Sara took Jonah's outstretched hand, climbing out of the ditch and over the fence. Jonah handed her luggage to Josh, who set it down on the other side. I got out of the ditch, but my luggage caught on a rock. Jonah picked it up and in one fluid motion, handed it to Josh. Josh struggled to get it to the ground as effortlessly as Jonah had gotten it off the ground. I couldn't help but be amazed at his strength. He offered me his hand, but I didn't need it. I climbed the fence and he followed.

We walked away from the fence, deeper into the property, toward the dirt road. The road rose gradually as we walked. Each of us dragged our suitcase, except Jonah, who had flung his duffel bag over his shoulder.

"How far to the house?" Sara asked.

"Less than a mile," East answered, her voice now calm.

East nudged her brother and pointed up the road. Two horses were running toward us. The horses were beautiful, white with brown markings. Like something out of an old movie. I had never been around horses, but watching them run took my breath away. The beauty was overwhelming. I watched in awe as they ran up to Jonah and East. Jonah placed his head against the head of the stallion. I could see the love between them. He then moved to the mare and placed his arms around her neck, giving her a hug of sorts. East petted them and clearly cared for them, and they for her, but it was Jonah who loved them.

"My brother is a horse whisperer," East said as the horses walked on either side of Jonah.

He placed his duffel bag on the stallion and kept it steady with his hand.

"We can see that," Sara said. "What are their names?"

"His name is Fulton. Her name is Talin," Jonah said.

"Those are interesting names," Blaise said.

Jonah petted Fulton. "I named him after Fulton Sheen. He was a bishop," Jonah said.

"And I named Talin. I thought it was a cool name. Not everyone puts as much thought into things as my brother does," East said, only half teasing.

"Maybe they should," Jonah said with an edge to his voice.

We reached the top of the small hill, and the house came into view. A two-story white farmhouse. Simple but nice. There was a large barn behind the house. It looked as though it had been white at one time, but now it matched the weathered gray look of the fence. The property was open in parts and heavily wooded in other parts. It was deeper than it was wide. It seemed to go forever.

"This is a lot of land," Josh said, looking from side to side.

He'd told me he grew up on a farm. I wondered if they had this much land.

"Our family has owned it for several generations. Most of the families around here are the same. There's another house at the far end of the property, that our grandparents live in. It's newer than ours, but smaller and not near the barn," East said.

"That's nice your grandparents live near you. I never knew any of mine," I said, unsure as to why I had shared that information.

Jonah turned to look at me. "I'm sorry," he said.

His sincerity made me uncomfortable. I wasn't used to that from strangers, or some of the people I knew best, for that matter.

As we approached, the door of the house opened and then closed. A few moments later, four people were running in our direction. Jonah and East dropped their bags and sprinted toward their family.

Jonah's bag fell from Fulton, who ran after Jonah. Josh picked it up and walked onward. He shifted it every now and then to relieve the strain. I dragged my suitcase with one hand and East's bag with the other. Sara took my purse.

In front of us was a clamor of greetings, hugging, and, no doubt, tears, though we were too far to see that or hear what was being said. We could hear the excitement.

As we neared I wondered who all the people were. There was a middle-aged woman with blonde hair and fair skin, no doubt their mom, by the way she hung on to both of them. A man in his late twenties or early thirties. He was shorter than Jonah and slightly thicker. He, too, was very good-looking. A young boy and an even younger girl. The woman eventually let go of Jonah and East. East scooped up the little girl, and the boy ran ahead of them as they walked back toward us.

The boy reached us first. "Hi, I'm JP. Who are all of you?" he said, looking at each of us.

We took turns telling him our names.

The rest of his family joined us as Blaise introduced herself.

"How do you spell your name?" JP asked.

Blaise told him.

"Are you named after Saint Blaise?" JP asked, alternating between standing on his tiptoes and flat feet. It seemed all he could do to keep from bouncing up and down.

"Hmm, you know, I don't know. My parents said they thought the name was cool. They never said if there was someone specific I was named for," Blaise answered, amused by his energy.

"Are you Catholic?" JP asked.

"John Paul, manners," the woman said, smiling at the boy.

Blaise looked at her. "It's okay," she said. She turned back to JP, who continued to bounce with his feet on the ground. "No, I'm not, but my mom was raised Catholic," she answered, looking down at the boy with kindness.

"Then I bet you're named for Saint Blaise. Don't you think she is, Mom?" JP asked the woman.

"Perhaps," his mom said as she ran her fingers through his sandy-blonde hair.

"Do you think we should introduce ourselves to our guests?" she asked the boy. She gazed at him with such love it made my heart hurt.

"I already did," he said, looking up at her.

"What about the rest of us?" she asked.

"Oh, yeah. You should introduce yourselves. I'm going to the barn to see if I can see Dad yet," he said, and in an instant he was running in the direction of the house and barn.

I was exhausted just watching him.

"Forgive my son. He has a lot of energy. His older brothers were the same way at this age, so there is hope, I suppose," she said, her gaze following her running son. "My name is Charlotte Page. This is our home and these are my kids. You know Jonah and East and, of course, John Paul is unforgettable. This is Eli," she said, gesturing to the man. "And this is my youngest, Quinn. Named after her father, who John Paul just ran to look for," Charlotte said, looking at the little girl clinging tightly to East.

Quinn could not be older than four, which meant Charlotte's kids spanned two-and-a-half decades. Most families I knew or saw had one or two kids and at most those two kids were four or five years apart, but more often they were two or three years apart. I had always looked at those families and thought they felt rushed. As if they had to have exactly the right number of kids in exactly the right number of years. But his woman had five kids, twenty-five years apart. There was no rush.

I focused on Quinn. She was almost an exact copy of East, except where East had light hair and eyes, Quinn had dark. Almost as dark as Blaise's.

"How old is she?" I asked.

"She's three, almost—" Charlotte's mouth fell open as she looked at me.

She stumbled backward, and Jonah caught her and steadied her.

"My God, Esther, it can't be you?" She stared at me in disbelief, leaning on Jonah as if she couldn't stand.

My knees buckled. Sara caught my arm and stared at me. She knew that name. Blaise and Josh looked from Charlotte to me; they also knew the name.

"Esther is my mom's name, but she died a long time ago," I said, wondering how this woman knew the name most sacred to me.

"Gabriella?" Charlotte blinked. Walking to me, she held my face in her hands.

Sara released my arm.

Charlotte moved her hands from my face and threw her arms around me. With her children, her cheeks had become damp with tears. With me, the tears fell so heavily they ran down her face, soaking my jacket.

I had no idea what was happening. This woman knew me … she knew my mom. How was this possible?

East walked to the other side of her mom, putting her arm around her, offering her both physical and emotional support. I stood motionless, trying to comprehend what was happening. Blaise and Josh joined Sara at my side.

"It's Bria's mom that you named me after, isn't it?" East asked her mom gently. "Your best friend who died before I was born."

Charlotte nodded and the tears continued to fall.

She knew my mom? Really knew my mom. Best friends. Named her daughter after her.

"Bria, honey, I'm your godmother," she said as she released me from her embrace. Her hands slid down my arms and landed on my hands, which she held tightly. East kept her hand on her mom's shoulder.

"I-I don't know … what to say," I answered, barely able to get the words out.

I knew nothing about my mom or my life with her. This woman knew her and had once been a part of our lives, an important part, from the sound of it. And I knew nothing of her existence. I had no idea I had a godmother. I felt so many emotions, but one distinct one was anger. Why had my father never told me about Charlotte? Why had I been made to feel as though he and I were completely alone in the world, when clearly this woman loved my mom and, based on her refusal to let go of my hands, loved me. Why did he do this to me? And if he had done this, what else had he done?

Five

It took me a moment to remember where I was. I blinked. I could see the setting sun through the bedroom window. JP had been asked to give up his room to Sara, Blaise, and me. I remember walking in a daze to the house and asking if there was somewhere I could lie down. JP took my hand and led me to his room. I was asleep almost before I got my shoes off. Sleep had always been how I dealt with things. Whenever life was too much, I went to sleep and stayed asleep for as long as I could. Sometimes I saw my mom in my dreams. Sometimes she comforted me. It was the only place I ever saw her. I had no pictures of her.

I heard the door open behind me. I wanted to turn to see who it was, but couldn't summon the strength. A moment later JP's nose was inches from my own. I blinked and jerked my head back.

"I knew you'd wake up soon," he said. "Come on, we're eating ice cream for dinner and you don't want to miss that."

He was right. I didn't. Hunger had woken me. A

hunger so intense I couldn't sleep through it. He grabbed my hand and pulled me up. I groaned.

"Don't worry, you can go back to bed soon. I go to bed at eight. What time do you go to bed?" he asked.

"Umm, I'm not sure. Do you know what time it is now?" I asked, straining to focus my mind. It wanted to sleep, but my body needed food.

"It's a little after five," he answered, still holding my hand and leading me out the door.

"How do you know?" I asked, shuffling slowly behind him.

He continued to pull me out of the room. "We have an old clock downstairs. The light didn't break it. Come on, let's go," he said.

"Can I stop at the bathroom first?"

"Sure, I'll show you where it is. You can only flush if you poop. That's what my mom said. And if you do flush, you have to use a scoop of water from the bucket to put into the back of the toilet. I'll show you," he said as we entered the bathroom.

Sitting in the bathtub with a large plastic cup next to it, a large bucket held what looked like pond water.

"How do you wash hands?" I asked. The dirty water in both the bucket and the toilet bowl made my stomach turn.

"We have hand sanitizer downstairs," he said before

running out of the room. Through the door I could hear him thumping down the stairs, shouting, "She's awake, she's awake."

The bathroom was decorated for young children. A towel with butterflies hung on a rack next to a towel with appliquéd dinosaurs, and two toothbrushes, one purple and one red, were in a yellow holder. I wondered now how we would brush our teeth or bathe. Things that were so easy yesterday had suddenly become difficult.

Glancing in the mirror before leaving the bathroom, I looked like I felt. I found a brush in one of the drawers and at least tamed my hair. I turned the faucet to wash my face, forgetting for a moment—nothing happened.

I left the bathroom in search of hand sanitizer. I went back to JP's room and found my purse, and inside it, my hand sanitizer next to my dead phone. Thoughts of my dad and Trent entered my mind and tears came to my eyes. I sat on JP's solar system comforter and looked out the large window framed by solar system curtains.

I could see Jonah outside, chopping firewood on one side of the barn. JP was running toward him. As I watched, he began loading some fallen pieces into a wheelbarrow. Sara stood nearby, no doubt flirting with Jonah. I shook my head. I dealt with stress by sleeping; she dealt with it by flirting. Neither was good, yet I couldn't help but think her way was less good.

On the other side of the barn East and Quinn pulled a red wagon with buckets in it, toward the house. I could see a line carved in the earth beyond the barn … a stream. That was our water supply. Josh and Blaise stood with Charlotte in a small fenced area between the house and the barn. I looked closer. It was a garden. That was our food supply, at least until the snow came. After that … I didn't know. Perhaps this would all be over by then.

* * *

The walls were lined with family photos. Children laughing in trees, children laughing in front of waterfalls, children laughing with horses and dogs. A picture of East in a white dress in a church. Similar pictures of each boy in a black suit at the same church. A picture of Eli in a long robe, in front of a rectangular table. I think it's called an altar. His family surrounding him, Quinn an infant in Charlotte's arms. JP, no older than Quinn is now.

I studied every picture. My dad had always been proud of the fact that I had never been in a church, never been "defiled by the lies," as he would say. Now I wondered if that was true. These people were religious; perhaps my mother had been too.

I stopped and stared. In a small silver picture frame I

saw myself. My mouth fell open and I couldn't breathe. This was my mother. I had never known how much I looked like her. I closed my eyes, but the tears poured forth anyway. I touched the glass between us, wishing she were real. I longed to feel her embrace.

My memories of how she looked had always been fuzzy. I was so young when she died and all the pictures had been lost in the fire.

I stood for a long while staring at that picture. Charlotte stood next to her in a cap and gown. Their arms around each other. It must have been Charlotte's college graduation. Both were so happy. My mother would have been almost the age I was now. I never felt pretty, but looking at my mother it was easy to say she was beautiful. The way her eyes glowed with joy, they illuminated her whole face, her whole being. I don't know that I have ever felt such joy.

I heard Eli and Quinn playing somewhere below. I forced my breath to deepen and slow. I forced the air deep into my lungs. I had to calm myself before going downstairs. I used my sleeves to wipe away the tears. I summoned what strength I had and walked down the stairs. I turned toward their voices and found myself in the kitchen. The appliances were simple. No stainless steel anywhere. The floor was a light-colored wood with a high sheen. It looked nothing like the white marble floors and stainless steel appliances of my father's kitchen.

It opened into a family room, and a small bar separated the two rooms. A fire glowed in the nearby fireplace, but I could feel no heat. I wondered if there were other fireplaces, other sources of heat. I hoped so.

Eli and Quinn sat coloring by the fireplace. Quinn was lucky to have brothers. I had always wanted one. Always wished I wasn't an only child. Above them two large guns—rifles—were lying awkwardly on the mantel, as if placed there quickly to keep the kids from reaching them. A man with graying hair, and the same muscular build as Jonah and Eli, sat on a couch near them, reading and taking notes on a yellow legal pad. It looked as if he were sketching a diagram of some sort.

I cleared my throat to announce my arrival.

"Good morning," Eli said, standing.

Quinn saw me and hid behind her brother. She was so shy, nothing like JP.

"Good evening," I said, my voice sounding strange to my ears. Tired and weak.

Quinn peeked out from her brother's side and looked at me. I wondered if she heard the strangeness.

The man walked toward me. "You really are your mother's twin," he said.

I did what I could to smile. Quinn watched me. I knew

she could see through me. I knew she knew I was about to burst into tears.

"Forgive me, I'm Quint. Charlotte's husband, your godfather." I could tell he wanted to give me a hug or in some way touch me to make sure I wasn't imagined. But he held back.

"Nice to meet you," I said, forcing myself to breathe—and not cry. I wanted to find Blaise or Sara or even Josh. I needed my friends. Needed their support in the twilight zone that had become our lives.

"This all must be so strange to you. You don't know us. Yet, you are like our lost daughter come home," he said, fighting back the emotion that emerged through his words.

I flinched when a door slammed shut somewhere nearby. JP ran into the room, followed by Jonah, East, and Sara.

"We're back. Is it time for ice cream yet?" JP asked, running to his dad.

"Almost. Go find your mom. She's in our room," Quint said, looking at his son.

"Okay." JP ran out of the room as quickly as he'd run in. He was like a force of nature. Nothing seemed to slow him.

I exhaled and looked at Sara. I begged her to help me, to get me out of this room and away from these people I didn't know, but who knew me.

She understood my expression. Jonah saw it too and looked away. East didn't notice. She looked only at Quinn, walking to her and taking her in her arms.

"Bria, will you come with me to find Blaise and Josh?" Sara asked.

I nodded, following her out of the room.

Next to the kitchen was a small hallway with a bench and lots of shoes. We stepped over the multitude of shoes that must have been JP's and went out the back door.

The air was cold, the sun setting. I zipped the thin running jacket; it offered almost no warmth. I crossed my arms around my body. Sara was silent as we walked toward the garden.

She must be exhausted. They all must be. The five or so hours I slept did little to alleviate the exhaustion. My legs felt like tree trunks beneath me, slowly, painfully moving forward. The cold assaulted me. I wanted to be in my warm apartment, sitting on the couch, cuddled in a blanket, watching a movie. Never again. I knew the answer to the question I didn't have the courage to ask. Never again would I have those things. Never again would anyone have those things.

Josh and Blaise looked up as we approached. The small gate of the garden slammed shut behind us.

Blaise and Josh walked toward us. "Hey, how are you?" she asked.

I burst into tears. "I saw a picture of my mom," I said between sobs.

Blaise and Sara both held me as I cried. I felt Josh's hand on my back. They were silent.

"What are you feeling?" Blaise asked, when I finally pulled away and wiped my eyes.

"I don't even know. It's all just so weird," I said once the tears stopped.

"You can say that again," Josh said.

"Josh!" Blaise said.

"What? It is totally weird. All of this is totally weird. The world as we know it ends and we are stranded with strangers who in fact are Bria's long-lost family she never knew she had. It's weird!" he said.

"Or fate," Sara said.

"What?" I sniffed.

"Like Josh said. This is weird, way too weird to be random," Sara said, looking at me.

I didn't know what she meant and didn't care. Not right now.

"Why didn't I know these people existed? That I had family down here? My dad always made it seem like the fire destroyed everything we had. Our house, our belongings …. my mom. He never said anything about anyone else being in our lives, about anyone else caring about me," I said, feeling the sense of betrayal rise within me.

"I'm sure he couldn't deal with it after your mom died," Josh said. The wind blew harder as he spoke. I pulled my thin running jacket tighter around my shivering body.

"That was eighteen years ago. It seems like at some point in the last eighteen years he should have told me I had godparents. That I had people who loved me," I said, almost whispering the last part.

I had always felt so alone in the world. My mom left me, not by choice, but by death. My father left me at the same time. If he felt any real love for me, he kept it hidden. He was around on nights and weekends. During the day I had nannies, some nicer than others. He always made sure someone was at my dance recital and gymnastic meet, but it was never him.

He blamed it on work. He was good at his job and was one of the highest-paid defense attorneys in the country. I followed some of his cases. I couldn't help but think that he was so well paid because he didn't care who he defended. Guilt or innocence, good or bad, meant nothing to him. If you could pay his fee, you could have him.

I always had the best clothes, went to the best schools,

had the most expensive cars. But the price I paid, or the price he made me think I had to pay for those things, was my dad. Now I wasn't so sure. I think that was the lie he told to justify his behavior. The truth was he didn't want to be around me.

"Until you guys entered my life, I never felt like anyone cared about me. And now these people say I'm their long-lost daughter. Quint almost cried when he saw me. You saw Charlotte's reaction when she saw me. They love me. Not for my stuff or how powerful my father is, but because I am part of their family. Their goddaughter. I feel like my life has been a lie. My father has lied to me, and I don't understand why. I feel betrayed by the one person who was never supposed to betray me."

"I'm sure when you're ready, Charlotte and Quint will answer any questions you have. If they knew you and your mom, they knew your dad too," Blaise said, her arm still around me.

I felt weak leaning on her, but I was too cold to pull away. "Maybe ... when I'm ready," I said.

* * *

It was dark as we walked back to the house in silence. The wind blew, the temperature was dropping. I was glad tonight we would have shelter.

The hallway by the back door was dark. A faint light glowed around the corner. The sound of family filled the space. A sound I'd only heard when visiting the houses of friends or on TV.

Everyone was in the kitchen and the family room. The rooms were lit by the fire and a few candles.

JP and Quinn were arguing over the chocolate ice cream. I didn't feel like eating, but I was starving. In twenty-four hours I'd had half a granola bar. Realizing that made me dizzy.

"Help yourselves. Even in the deep freeze this was already getting soft. We might as well eat it while we have the chance," Charlotte said as she sat with her bowl of ice cream on one of the bar stools at the kitchen counter.

Several different types of ice cream sat in the kitchen sink. Someone had laid out four bowls, four spoons, and four glasses for us.

"We boiled some water. It's in that pitcher if you want any," Quint said from his place at the kitchen table.

"Thank you. This is very nice of you," Blaise answered. She poured four glasses of water, handing one to each of us. I didn't realize how thirsty I was until the moment the water hit my lips. Once it started I couldn't stop. The thirst overpowered me. I filled another glass and drank half of it before the thirst was tolerable.

"Thank you for letting us stay here," I said, my voice cracking. I lowered my head to look at the ice cream. I stood between Blaise and Sara.

Blaise put her hand on my back. "We were lucky to meet Jonah and East on the road. It's difficult to imagine where we would be if we hadn't," she said.

"Luck had nothing to do with it," East said from her spot at the table.

"What do you mean?" I asked, wondering if East and Sara had been talking.

"There's no way all of this is random. It's not just coincidence that the only car on the highway within miles of us happened to have the daughter of my mom's best friend in it. The daughter she hadn't seen in eighteen years," East said, spoon in hand, looking at me, her tone harsh.

"I don't know how it could be anything but coincidence. It's not like I arranged all of this." I felt heat rise to my cheeks.

"Relax, Bri. She meant it wasn't coincidence, it was God," Sara said, scooping the last bit of strawberry ice cream into her bowl.

"Oh," I said. "That seems even more unlikely than me setting all this up," I said under my breath as I scooped rocky road into a bowl. Only Charlotte was close enough to hear. She looked at me as I scooped, but said nothing.

I sat next to her. Sara took a seat at the kitchen table; I knew she would. There was an empty one next to Jonah. Blaise and Josh sat beside me.

"What should we have tomorrow for dinner? Chocolate cake?" Eli teased JP.

They were making the best of the situation. I knew this, but it bothered me. It was as if they were making light of it all. As if it were a temporary power outage and not what it was.

"I was thinking tomorrow we could do Thanksgiving. Or some version of it. We have the turkey and casseroles made up in the fridge. I was too distracted today to think about them, but we have to eat them tomorrow or throw them out," Charlotte said, turning her body toward her family as she spoke.

"How will we cook things?" East asked.

There was silence for a moment. I couldn't help but wonder how we would do most of the things we had done before.

"What if we made a sort of oven to go on top of the fire pit?" Jonah suggested. He was leaning toward Eli as he spoke. Sara sat so close to him he didn't have much choice.

"That could work. What would we use to make it?" Eli asked.

"We could take the inside drum out of the washing machine," Quint said.

Charlotte spun on her barstool to face the table. "The washing machine?" Charlotte sounded confused.

Quint looked at her. "Why not? It's not like it's going to be washing any clothes now," Quint said. "And we need an oven."

Charlotte turned back to her bowl of ice cream. She took another bite. "I guess," she mumbled.

The three Page men, Sara, and East spent the rest of dinner discussing how to best disassemble the washing machine and turn it into an oven. The rest of us stayed out of the conversation. I focused on my ice cream, trying to forever remember the taste of chocolate and marshmallows. I wondered if I would ever eat rocky road ice cream again. Sugar, dairy, everything I had taken for granted were now things I would probably never have again.

Charlotte sat silent next to me. I imagined she was trying not to be upset about the destruction of her washing machine and, probably more than that, trying not to be upset that what had once been important to her daily life no longer was.

After my third helping of ice cream, Quinn left her place at the table and walked over to Charlotte.

"Momma," her little voice squeaked, "I want to go to bed."

"Not me!" JP announced as he jumped up from his spot at the table and threw his bowl in the sink.

"I know, JP, not you. But you at least need to come with me to get your pajamas on and brush your teeth," Charlotte said.

"Will you all see what you can do with the dishes and trash? And remember, the soap we have is all we have," Charlotte said, looking at her family.

They nodded.

Charlotte and her youngest children disappeared up the stairs, taking a candle with them.

"Can we do anything to help?" Sara asked, still leaning toward Jonah.

Quint shook his head. "I'm not sure what can be done tonight. We need more water to boil before we wash the dishes. And the trash—I guess we will bury it."

"Dad! We can't bury trash," East exclaimed.

"What do you think they do at landfills?" Jonah crossed his arms and leaned back in his chair.

"So, that doesn't make it right. What are we going to do, turn our yard into a waste dump?" East retorted.

Jonah leaned forward. Sara leaned back, away from Jonah. I could sense the anger in him from across the room.

I knew she could too.

"You get that the trash we have now is the only trash we will ever have, right? That we aren't going to the store and buying more stuff? There will never be more cartons of ice cream or empty boxes of hair dye? You get all that, right?" His words were angry and sarcastic.

East pushed back from the table. "Shut up, Jonah. I get that you are just as depressing to be around as you've always been." She put her bowl in the sink and stomped upstairs.

"That was uncalled for," Quint said after she'd gone.

"What was? What did I say that was wrong or untrue?" Jonah said, glaring at the wall behind where his sister had been sitting.

"Your tone, that's what was uncalled for. I know you're an adult, but you are my son and East is my daughter, and no man, especially not my son, is going to speak to my daughter that way," Quint said, fully in control of his emotions. Fully aware he was in the right.

"Fine. I'm sorry. But I'm sick of her not getting how serious this is. This is not a power outage. This is going back in time two hundred years and none of us knows how to survive in that world."

I could hear the scared child that still lived in his heart—that still lived in mine too, if I was honest. I was terrified of this and had no idea what to think, let alone what to do.

"Son, East knows how serious this is. We all know how serious this is. Well, maybe not John Paul," he said with a slight lightness to his voice, "but even Quinn is shaken. It's true that East wants to go into town and see if others know anything."

Jonah started to interrupt.

"And I know you vehemently disagree with that idea," Quint responded before Jonah could. "I don't disagree with you. But that's her love for others. She wants to make sure others in the community are okay. I respect her for that. Your mom and I will keep discussing options. But one thing Mom and I both know is we will do whatever it takes to keep you kids safe. Your safety,"—he paused and exhaled, locking eyes with Jonah—"your survival is everything to us."

"I know," Jonah said, nodding, blinking tears from his eyes. "And you know we feel the same way about you and Mom."

"I know you do, and I couldn't love you more for it. All of you," he said, looking at Eli, who sat silently watching the exchange between his father and brother.

After a short pause, Eli said, "We need to get Nonie and Pops. They can't stay at their house alone. Not now."

I remembered now East saying her grandparents lived on the property.

"Mom and I already decided we will bring them here tomorrow. Kicking and screaming, if need be," Quint said.

"This house is going to be overflowing," Eli said, his gaze going from the family room back to the kitchen.

"Sorry. We don't mean to take away room and food from your family. We can leave," I said, knowing we had nowhere else to go.

"First of all, Bria, you are family," Eli said with kindness in his voice. "And second of all, you misunderstood. I didn't mean it as a bad thing. More of my cup runneth over sort of thing."

"But Bria's right," Josh said. "By us being with you, we will take away resources from your family."

"There is nothing more precious than life. That includes the life of each of you. You will stay and we will figure things out." Quint's tone was firm.

"Besides, there is safety in numbers," Jonah said, looking first at Josh and then at me, his voice back to normal. "The food we have will only last so long. After that, we'll have to get a lot more creative."

Sara looked at Quint. "How long do you think this will last?" she asked.

Jonah and Eli exchanged glances. I got the sense they

knew something but didn't want to tell her … to tell us.

Quint leaned back from the table and looked at each of us in turn, before stopping at Sara and answering her question. "I'm not sure. I know the world has changed, categorically changed. What we once took for granted, clean drinking water coming into our homes, food in abundance, heat,"—his voice became soft—"and safety, those things no longer exist as they once did. It is possible with time, those things could exist again. Certainly, the infrastructure and the knowledge exist."

"So you agree with Jonah that it was an electromagnetic pulse?" Blaise asked.

Jonah and Eli looked at each other again. There was a pause and then Quint spoke.

"Last night I couldn't sleep. East sent me a text at eleven, saying they were a hundred fifty miles out. I expected them by two at the latest, so I was waiting up. I can't sleep when I know my kids are traveling. I would have been doubly worried had I known Eli was on his way."

"That's why I didn't tell you," Eli said, interrupting.

"You're a good boy, but I would rather know the truth than be naïvely unconcerned," Quint said, looking at both his sons in turn.

"Anyway, I was watching TV to distract myself. A few minutes before one o'clock the show was interrupted. The announcer was panicked, not calm and put together like you normally see them. It was clear there was no script. There had been no makeup or hair done. He was not anyone I recognized. Perhaps the camera guy or whoever happened to be there. He said the U.S. was under attack. That several large weapons were headed for us. He said the air force and navy were trying to intercept, but there was a problem. He didn't say what it was. He said to remain calm and in our homes. Then the picture cut out.

"Immediately after that, a light shone through every window in the house. Everything went dark. Charlotte and the kids stayed asleep. I locked the doors, got my hunting rifle down and loaded, got on my knees and prayed. Just before dawn Eli knocked on the door. I soaked the poor kid's shirt with my tears. I woke Charlotte and told her what happened. She was almost inconsolable, knowing Jonah and East were stranded somewhere. But I knew they were close. I had faith they would make it. I had to. Eli stayed with his mom as she cried. He prayed when she couldn't. I made sure everything around the house looked okay, and then I had to check on my parents. I tried to get them to come back with me and they refused. I came back, and you all were here. I can't tell you how relieved I was to have all my kids with me. When I heard Bria had come home too,"—his voice cracked. He pinched the bridge of his nose and sniffed back tears.

Quint cleared his throat and then continued. "I suppose then, Blaise, the answer to your question is I don't know what it was, but I know it was an attack and there were several weapons. I know our government was unable to stop them, and I would think that means the government and the armed forces were caught off guard. Based on the fact that none of our electronics are working, I would say, yes, it was an EMP, or more accurately, several very large EMPs detonated in the upper atmosphere to have the most effect."

No one spoke. I stared at the small cross on the wall behind Jonah. I thought of my father and longed for him to be with me. I didn't care that he hadn't been honest with me. I missed him.

"Did the announcer say who was attacking us?" Josh asked. His words were slow and methodical, as if it was a struggle to get them out.

Quint looked from Josh to Blaise, and shook his head no.

Josh exhaled. We'd all been worried the answer would be China, and Blaise would become a target.

"Are there actual attackers or terrorists or whatever on the ground, like in the cities?" Sara asked. I knew her thoughts were of her mother and sister.

Quint looked at Sara. "I don't know, but it seems unlikely to me that someone, some entity, would go to the trouble of setting off EMPs just to set them off. There had to be a bigger reason."

A chill surged through me. Our country had been debilitated and no one saw it coming. We had been naïvely unconcerned, as Quint said. How did this happen? How could this happen? How would we survive?

We sat in silence. Josh held Blaise tightly to his chest. The rest of us made no attempts to comfort one another. What could be said? What could be done?

Quint looked up as footsteps approached from the stairs.

"What are you all talking about?" Charlotte said, holding the hand of a wide-awake JP.

"The events of the last day," Quint said stoically.

Charlotte nodded. "As the mother of the house, I announce that it is time for bed. None of you slept last night. Not to mention we have a lot to do tomorrow and we only have so many candles."

Jonah looked up at his mother and then down at his hands. "Where is East? I need to tell her something," he said.

"Upstairs with Quinn," Charlotte said, looking at her son.

"Quinn was too scared to sleep without her," JP said, in a tone mocking his little sister.

"Yes, and you will be sleeping with Dad and me, so it is perfectly fine for Quinn to want to sleep with her big sister," Charlotte said, giving JP a look that said, *Don't you dare tease your sister*. "Jonah, she forgives you. She told me about what happened and she knows you are stressed. We all are."

Jonah nodded and continued looking at his hands.

"Do you four need anything? Josh, the boys can get a sleeping bag for you. You girls have John Paul's bed and Eli can get you a sleeping bag. Sorry we can't offer actual beds to all of you," Charlotte said.

Josh stood next to Blaise, and said, "You've done more than enough."

"Thank you for saving us," Blaise said. She stood and gave Charlotte a hug, tears in her eyes.

Charlotte hugged her back. "You three are part of our family now. Bria already was, but the rest of you are, also. We will work as a family and get through this," she said, squeezing Blaise's hand.

Blaise nodded and bit her lip to keep from crying.

Six

I awoke, disoriented. It was dark and cold. Moonlight shone through the large window in JP's room. There had been no reason to close the drapes. The sun had set long before we had laid down. With the drapes open, cold air seemed to pour in from the closed windows. I shivered violently under the covers. I could hear the soft breathing of Sara and Blaise on the bed above me. I had insisted on the floor, but now I wished I hadn't. The bed must be warmer than the floor. My body ached for more sleep. I pulled the blankets over my head, hoping my breath would warm the air around me enough so I could fall back asleep. I pulled my knees to my chest and tried to warm my toes. They felt like ice, even with socks on.

How was this going to work? It was only November; the first frost hadn't come yet. It was still getting up to the seventies during the day. How was I going to survive winter? How were any of us?

I sat up. My body shivered as I crept to my suitcase. I layered on as many clothes as I could. I spread my blanket gently over my sleeping friends. I walked out of the room and tiptoed down the stairs. It was too dark to see the picture of my mother, though I stopped and looked in its direction when I was close to it. I sighed and walked to the family room.

The fire was burning brightly. Eli sat beside it, a string of brown beads in his hand. I looked at the rifles still on the mantel above him. I looked back at Eli. Did he wake up early or was he on watch?

He looked up as I entered. "Couldn't sleep?"

"I tried, but I was a little cold," I answered, not wanting to appear ungrateful for the room I shared with my friends. I sat on the ground as close to the fire as I could without getting burned. Half awake, half asleep.

He nodded and moved his fingers along the beads. After a moment he put the beads in his pocket. "The house was designed for central heat and air. It doesn't matter how warm the fire is. The rest of the house won't feel its heat," he said.

I yawned. "Maybe I'll sleep down here tonight," I said.

He looked toward the drawn curtains. "I think we will all be sleeping down here soon," he said.

"Do you know what time it is?" I asked.

He nodded. "A little after five."

I groaned.

"You aren't a morning person?" he teased.

"I don't believe people should wake up before the sun," I mumbled as I lay my head on my knees.

"You know, as a baby you were up at five almost every day. I remember your parents coming over for dinner and falling asleep on the couch while you and Jonah played right there," he said, pointing to the middle of the large rug I sat on.

I felt a mixture of joy and pain at his words. I turned my head to look at him. "What was my mom like?" I asked.

He raised his head to the ceiling and thought for a moment. "She was joyful. I suppose that's the best way to describe her. She loved life. Loved you and your dad. Loved us. Loved God. And the love was there in all she did. From the smallest act to the largest. She wasn't always happy, but she was always joyful. She made me want to be like her," he said, smiling down at me.

"Until yesterday, I'd never met anyone who knew her—well, except my father, and he never talks about her. I never knew she was religious or that she looked like me. I knew she loved me. That much I could remember. I remember the joy I felt with her, so it makes sense that you describe her as joyful," I said, feeling oddly at peace about speaking of my mother.

"Did your dad not raise you in the church?" Eli asked, looking puzzled.

"What church? But no, he hates religion. He's the most vocal atheist I know. And I know several."

"I see. And what do you think?" Eli asked, his voice relaxed yet interested.

"I don't know what I think. I've never been to church, never celebrated religious things. My father did all he could to keep me free of lies, as he called it. But finding out my mom was religious makes me question things," I said, lifting my head and looking at him.

"Your mom and your dad, for that matter, were devout Catholics. It's actually partly because of your mom that I became a priest," he said with a distant look in his eyes.

"You're a priest?"

He nodded.

"That's cool," I said, putting my head back down to my knees. The heat of the fire washing over me reminded me I was tired.

"I think so," he said, pausing as if thinking about something. "Bria, where did you and your dad go? It was like you vanished."

I could hear the pain in his voice. I looked at him, sensing he had missed me as much as his parents. "DC. It's where I grew up," I said.

"Holt Ford in Washington? He always hated cities. I

can't imagine him in a city that size," he said.

"He seemed at home to me," I said, my eyes closed again. I wanted to sleep.

"Why did you leave so quickly? My parents went over the day after the funeral to check on you and your dad, and you were gone. They tried to find your dad, tried to find you, but until yesterday we had no idea what happened," he said, the hurt noticeable in his voice.

I opened my eyes a little. "Where did they go?" I asked, feeling confused.

"Your house," he said.

"My house was destroyed in the fire," I said, gazing sleepily at Eli. His expression changed into one of confusion. I raised my head and stared at him.

I heard footsteps on the stairs.

"We wondered where you went," Sara said as she and Blaise walked into the room and sat next to me in front of the fire.

"Aww, this is better. That room was freezing!" Blaise said.

"Sorry if we're interrupting," Sara said as she looked at me staring at Eli. His face still showed confusion.

He blinked and his expression returned to normal. "No, we were just reminiscing. Or at least I was. I was remembering Bria as an energetic toddler playing on this rug. But I guess it's time to get the day started. I'm sure Mom and Dad are up by now. They are probably trying to be quiet so they don't wake John Paul. Once that boy's eyes open, he's awake and there is no slowing him down until he passes out at night," Eli said as he stood and stretched his back.

I watched him walk away. I wondered why he had looked so confused. I wondered what he was not telling me.

"You sure we didn't interrupt something?" Sara said, teasing me after Eli left the room.

"You interrupted something, but not what you're thinking," I said, irritated that Sara had assumed I was flirting with Eli. She always assumed everyone was flirting, probably because she was always flirting.

"So what did we interrupt?" Blaise asked.

"He said my mom was joyful and religious," I answered.

"Your mom was religious? Weird. I wonder what your dad thought of that," Sara said, holding her hands out toward the fire.

"Probably that she was crazy," Josh said, entering the room. He sat down by Blaise and pulled her into him.

"No," I said. "He said my father was religious too. He said it was because of my mom that he became a priest."

"Your dad was religious?" Blaise asked, shock in her voice.

"Eli's a priest?" Sara asked, horror in her voice.

"Yes and yes," I answered.

"That is weird," Josh said.

"Which one?" I asked.

"Both. Your dad is the most anti-God person I know, and it is totally weird that Eli's a priest," Josh said, holding on tightly to Blaise.

"My dad is not anti-God," I said, feeling defensive, though I didn't know why.

"Your dad! Your dad thinks all people who have faith are naïve, brainwashed, superstitious, or stupid, or all of the above," Sara said in her "don't try me" voice.

"No, he doesn't," I said, only half believing my own words.

Blaise frowned and said, "Bria, don't lie. You know that's exactly what he thinks. He has told all of us that and he didn't care that Sara and I were leaving to go to church when he went on and on about why God doesn't exist."

"Okay, fine, that's what he thinks." I had heard that and much worse from my father throughout my lifetime. "Eli also said my father and I just disappeared. His parents looked for us and had no idea until yesterday what happened to us," I said, no longer interested in discussing my father's religious, or anti-religious, beliefs.

"That's kind of creepy," Josh said.

"What is?" I asked.

"You and your dad disappearing. It's like he kidnapped you or something. Then he told you there was no one else in your life, but clearly these people were in your life," Josh said, leaning toward the fire.

"What if he was trying to protect her?" Blaise whispered. "What if the Pages are no good and he didn't want them to know where Bria was?" Her eyes had widened.

"What are you all whispering about?" Charlotte said cheerfully as she walked toward the fire. We all jumped when we saw her.

Without missing a beat, Sara said, "How cold JP's room is. We don't want to be unkind, but it was freezing."

"I know. Our room was freezing too. Perhaps tonight we will camp out in here," she said, looking from couch to floor as if trying to figure out where everyone would sleep.

* * *

The sun was beginning to shine through the windows. John Paul announced his arrival by hopping into the room like a frog. Quint stumbled after him.

"Do we have a plan for the day?" Eli asked following his dad into the room.

"We need to figure out how to cook, and we also need more water to drink and clean with," Charlotte said. She was wide awake.

I bet she didn't drink coffee. She was too awake, too early in the day. Quint, on the other hand, looked half asleep.

"We also have to get Mom and Dad to leave their house and come stay with us," Quint said, his words coming slower than he had probably intended.

"In other words, we have to do the impossible," East said. She was carrying a sleepy Quinn into the room.

When Quinn saw her mom she reached out her hands. Charlotte took her tired girl and sat on the hearth.

"Are you cold, sweetie?"

Quinn nodded.

East came and stood in front of the fire. "I held her to me all night, but it was still really cold," she said.

"I know. I snuggled with John Paul and Dad all night and we were all still a little chilly. I think tonight we will all be sleeping by the fire," Charlotte said, petting Quinn's hair.

Sara leaned her head next to mine. "I wonder where Jonah is," she whispered.

I looked around. He was the only one missing. I shrugged.

"You think he's still asleep?" she whispered.

He didn't strike me as the sleeping-in type. I shrugged again. Sara bit her lip and looked around. She was so into him. I put my head down and rolled my eyes.

From across the room, Eli said, "Josh, will you help me grab the cooler from the back porch? Last night Mom put all the food in it that needed to be refrigerated."

Josh stood and followed Eli out.

They returned a few moments later carrying a large cooler, setting it on the floor near the kitchen table.

"Quinn and John Paul, do you want some yogurt? It might be the last you get for a while," Quint said.

"The kids love yogurt," East said quietly to Blaise, Sara, and me. "This is going to be hard on them. Once it really sets in," she said, standing to get something to eat.

"It's going to be hard on all of us," I said under my breath as I stood and stepped toward the cooler.

The cold night had kept the food colder than the lukewarm fridge would have. Casseroles lined the bottom. Other things like yogurt, cheese, and milk were near the top.

At Charlotte's urging, Quinn and JP each ate two yogurts. Her worry for them was palpable, though she tried to hide it.

Looking at her and her family, I knew my father had not taken me from them because they were bad. Rather, it seemed because they were good. They appeared, from my point of view, to be the perfect family. Perfect in the sense of their love for one another. They each put the other's needs before their own. They exemplified what I thought a family should be. Charlotte, in particular, made me wonder what life would have been like growing up with a mom who loved me, who cared about me, who wanted to spend time with me. I was envious of her kids.

After breakfast, chores were divided up. Josh and Blaise were to weed the garden and harvest what had to be harvested. With the garden now a primary source of food, its productiveness mattered a great deal more than it once had. East, JP, and Sara were told to do what they could to construct an outdoor oven and start cooking our Thanksgiving feast. The rest of us were assigned to, as East called it, the impossible task of getting Quint's parents to consent to come and stay at the main house. I was asked to accompany them because, Quint thought the shock of seeing me may confuse them enough to get them to come. After the third time Sara asked me where I thought Jonah was, I started to wonder. He never appeared.

* * *

My mind drifted as I rode Talin across the property. There was a path, not quite a dirt road, through the field. A car had driven this way more than once. Eli held the reins as he walked next to us. I had never ridden a horse before. It was soothing. Part of me wanted to tell Eli to let go so I could control her, but I was afraid I was overestimating my abilities. Charlotte rode Fulton next to me. Quint walked in front of us, with a pistol stuck between his belt and his jeans. He had left the hunting rifles at the house with East. I didn't hear the conversation, but I knew protecting the family was Quint's top priority.

Quint, Eli, and Charlotte talked now and then about ways to try and convince Nonie and Pops they had to leave. I heard repeatedly that it wasn't safe for them to live alone, but Charlotte said that wouldn't matter to them. Eli suggested the tactic of how much they'd be contributing to the family and how needed they were. Quint stated more than once that if he had to literally tie them to the horses, he'd do it.

I could see the smoke rising from their chimney, blowing in the wind above the tree line. As we came through the small patch of trees that seemed to separate their part of the land from the rest of the property, a small house came into sight. In a small, screened back porch a woman with curly white hair sat reading, a blanket wrapped around her. She put the book down and walked outside to greet us. An elderly man rolled out onto the porch. Nobody had mentioned he was in a wheelchair. Any sort of difference would have been immediately noted in the world I grew up in. But that was apparently not the case here.

On the brick walkway that went halfway to the trees, Pops followed behind Nonie. His skin was brown like leather; hers was plump and ghostly white. The lines on both their faces were deep and soft. I never saw those kinds of lines in New York or DC. It was comforting, in an odd way, to see them. To me it meant Nonie and Pops weren't afraid to age. Unlike so many others I knew they didn't seem to believe their ideal self existed decades before, but rather, right now.

Nonie hugged her son and grandson. Charlotte slid gracefully off Fulton. I was afraid to try. I decided to wait until someone offered to help me down, so I sat unmoving atop Talin.

It was Pops who noticed me first, noticed that I wasn't East. The shock on his face caught me off guard. I turned to look behind me to see what had scared him so badly, and realized it was me. The twin of my dead mother. Nonie took a step back when her eyes met mine.

"This is Esther's daughter, Gabriella. Jonah and East met her and her friends on the highway," Charlotte said, reaching out to take Nonie's hand to keep her steady.

"Jonah and East are home?" Pops said, choking back tears.

"They made it home while I was here yesterday," Quint said, also full of emotion.

"Thank God," Nonie said, giving Charlotte a hug.

Pops pulled a white handkerchief from his pants pocket and wiped the tears from his cheeks.

Soon their eyes returned to me. I felt self-conscious. I wanted to get out of sight. I tried to emulate Charlotte's graceful dismount and fell hard on my butt.

Eli rushed to help me up. "Are you okay?" he asked. "That looked like it hurt."

"It did," I said, brushing the dirt from my tunic. I put my head against Talin's neck. I wanted to hide.

Nonie walked around Talin and embraced me.

"We have missed you so much. When you and your father disappeared, it was as if we lost your mother and brother all over again," she said.

My head jerked. "My brother?" I said, searching her eyes for some indication that she had not meant to say the word.

Charlotte came around and stood by Eli. I leaned against Talin for support.

"Don't you remember?" Charlotte asked me.

"Remember what?"

"Your mom was pregnant when she died," Eli said,

reaching out to take my hand as I slid down Talin and sat on the ground.

"Pregnant?" I said, staring up at them.

"Bria, how do you think your mom died?" Eli said, kneeling beside me.

"A fire. It burned down our house. She told my dad to get me out, but she never made it out," I said, barely able to get the words out.

Eli looked at his mom, and then me. "There was no fire," he said, holding my hand with both of his.

It was my tether to this world. Without his physical touch, my mind would have fled. None of this made sense.

"Your mom died giving birth to your brother. Neither one of them survived," Charlotte said as she knelt beside me on the wet ground.

Images swirled in my mind. My mother with a swollen stomach, hugging me and laughing. Me, placing a sticker of a gray elephant on a blue wall. Putting my hand on her belly and feeling something hit my hand. My mother laughing at my reaction. My mother in a hospital bed. Her squeezing my hand, telling me it will be okay and to go with Aunt Charlotte. Crying for my mother in Charlotte's arms. A warm tear, not my own, falling on my cold arm. My father's face so broken, so altered. Quint, holding me as Charlotte sobbed. Quint, telling me my mom had gone to heaven with my little brother. My mother, lying down. Me, running to her. Touching her. Her skin hard. My father, picking me up as I screamed and fought his stone arms—fought to get back to her. His grip was hard and silent. Crying as my father filled suitcases with my clothes and his, but not my mother's. Waking up in the car, hearing nothing but the tires against the highway.

I held Charlotte with all the strength I had. I was afraid if I let her go I would disappear. Stop existing. I didn't feel real. But Charlotte did. This woman who knew the past that I only had glimpses of. She felt real. For a moment I felt like I did when I was a child, scared of a thunderstorm, being held tightly by my mother.

Seven

I stayed in her arms for what felt like hours. She held me closest when my sobbing was most intense and loosened her arms when I was calmer. I felt love. And I cried harder, realizing how much I missed it and for all I had done trying to find it. I cried for my mother. For the little brother I never knew I had. For the realization that there was no way my mother could love me after what I'd done, the choices I'd made. She who had died for her unborn child. I cried as I felt the hatred for myself more than I felt the loss of my mother. With hatred came anger, not at me, but at my father.

"Why did he lie to me?" I asked, letting go of Charlotte and wiping my face.

We were alone. Talin stood by me. I felt her breath as she turned her head at the sound of my voice.

"I don't know," Charlotte said. I could hear the confusion and sorrow in her voice.

"My whole life has been a lie." I stared into her eyes … searching for something, anything that would explain why he would do that to me.

Her eyes held no answers. "I know," she said.

We sat in silence.

* * *

Quint appeared above us. "I'm sorry, but we need Talin," he said.

I wondered what I looked like to him, my eyes swollen, cheeks wet.

I didn't want her to go; her presence comforted me.

"Why?" Charlotte asked, irritation in her voice. She seemed to know how I felt about Talin.

"We turned Dad's pickup into a sort of wagon. We're going to use Fulton and Talin to pull it," Quint answered, picking up Talin's reins.

"They've agreed to come?" Charlotte asked.

"Eli and I didn't give them a choice. To be honest, I think they were both so shocked to see Gabriella that it knocked the stubbornness out of them. At least for the moment," Quint said, taking Talin's reins and pulling her toward the side of the house. She fought him for a second and turned to look at me. I nodded my head toward Quint, and she walked away with him.

Thinking out loud more than talking to me, Charlotte said, "I suppose if there is any good to come out of this day, it's that they agreed to come. I was so worried about them out here by themselves."

"What were you worried about?" I asked, relieved the memories had stopped for the moment.

"A million things. How would they get water? Food? What if they got hurt? But more than any of that, I suppose I was scared for them, as I am for all of us, about what happens when everyone else runs out of water and food. What happens now, when there is no law, no government to speak of? Our way of life is gone. We can't let that change who we are, our moral code, but we can't be naïve and think it won't change others. Or perhaps it won't change them; it will simply set them free to be who they have always been."

"You're scaring me," I said, looking into her eyes. She had seemed so calm and easygoing, but I wondered now if I knew her at all.

"Tragedies change people. Look at your dad."

I winced at the mention of him. I didn't want to talk about him.

"He was Eli's godfather. He was like a brother to us. Quint's best friend. He loved God, loved the church. Loved us. And he left all of that. He turned his back on all of us. He took you from us. Do you know how long we looked for you? How we prayed every day for you and for him? I never would've thought he could do the things he did. And yet he did. So if that's what someone I know, someone I love, can do, imagine what others are capable of. The reality is that we are all capable of causing the world great joy or great pain. Our choices, our everyday, ordinary choices create who we become and how we are in the world. The great villains of humanity did not wake up one day and after a life of good, decide to commit mass murder. It was their choices day in and day out that led them to those moments."

"And yet," she said, her gaze focused on me, "we have the example of your dad who, day in and day out, chose good, and still he fell. So then, in this moment where the world is redefined, what will happen? How many people who chose good every day before today, will fall? They will fall to save themselves. Fall to save their families. Fall because they have no hope. How many others who have chosen small acts of evil day after day will choose large acts of evil? Perhaps to save themselves, perhaps because they know they can and there will be no societal retribution. Either way, the world just got a great deal scarier."

I shivered, not from the cold, but from her words.

She continued. "We will survive only by recognizing the realities of the world we now live in. I want those I love with me at all times. I want to have eyes on them, to know they are safe. I know that will not always be possible, but having Nonie and Pops with us means not only will I have them with me, but no one else I love will leave to check on them. People knew they lived here alone. It was only a matter of time before someone came to take what they could." She looked beyond her property, staring into the distance. Staring at some unnamed force lurking, waiting to hurt her family.

I looked at her and said, "This is a small community, right? There can't be that much badness here." I didn't believe in good or evil. Those words meant that one choice was inherently better than another and my father had explained many times how intrinsic values did not exist. Cultures determined values. I wondered, though, if he was right. Certain things in life, certain choices, did seem to be innately good or evil.

Charlotte shook her head and said, "It's not quite small enough that we know everyone. I'm sure it seemed that way to you, but if you go farther east, you will come to an actual town. Go another hour either east or south and you will come to larger cities. It is only a matter of time before people from the towns and cities come into the country looking for resources. We are blessed we live in such a remote part of the country. God only knows what's happening in the urban areas."

My whole body shuddered at the thought of the urban areas. They contained my dad, Sara's mom, Sara's little sister, Trent, and countless others I knew.

Charlotte's gaze shifted away from my eyes. I turned following her gaze.

The two horses were connected with large ropes and belts to a red Ford pickup truck. Eli and Quint walked in front of them, holding their reins. Pops sat behind the steering wheel and Nonie sat beside him. Piled in the truck and truck bed were what seemed to be all of their belongings. In actuality, it was probably only those items that were either most precious or most useful. A small metal cage with chickens inside was tied on top of the pile.

Charlotte and I stood and walked toward Eli and Quint. The wet ground made the jeans and tunic I'd been wearing for two days cling to my body.

"You'll have to walk and talk," Quint said, holding onto Talin's reins. "I don't want to stop the horses. It was tough for them to get the truck moving. Eli had to help push."

"Did Nonie and Pops get everything they wanted? Did you get all of the food? Water? Weapons? Ammunition? Matches? Blankets?" Charlotte asked in rapid succession.

"No, and I think yes to everything else. Go talk to Mom. You can ask her," Quint said, keeping a steady pace. Eli walked next to him, holding Fulton's reins.

Charlotte hurried to the truck.

I walked beside Talin and petted her from time to time.

94

We followed the dirt road back to the Pages' house. No doubt this truck had come this way many times before, though never pulled by horses.

"Are you doing okay?" Quint asked, peering around Talin to look at me.

"I guess so," I said, trying not to think.

"It's a lot to deal with," he said.

"Yeah, it is," I said, leaning my head against Talin, partly for her support, partly to hide from Quint and Eli. I didn't want to talk about anything. I wanted to sleep, but knew I couldn't.

* * *

We came to the flat, wooden bridge that crossed the stream. JP saw us from his place at the fire. He ran to meet us. I could smell the turkey cooking. The smell of the rolls was intoxicating. I knew I would miss wheat the most. This would be our last real meal. From now on it would be a mixture of something we killed and something we grew, if the frost held out. Charlotte was the mother of five. She had a large pantry and there were lots of dry goods in it, but those would be saved for winter. I hoped the truck behind me also carried food. There were thirteen of us now, including Quinn and JP. Not to mention the horses and chickens. Gathering food for all of us would not be easy.

Quint and Eli led the horses toward the house. We passed Blaise, Josh, Sara, and East sitting at the fire pit, which had a large flat piece of metal arched over it. They'd made a sort of oven. They waved as we went by. I waved back, but had no desire to talk to anyone. I wanted only to be with Talin. Her calm presence soothed me. I needed her next to me.

Jonah and Quinn came out of the house. When Quinn saw her mom, she ran to her. Charlotte scooped her up and hugged her tightly against her. I understood why Charlotte was so adamant that her family be together. She loved deeply; she had much to lose.

Jonah took Fulton's reins from Eli. He leaned his head against Fulton and rubbed his neck.

"Do you mind taking Talin?" Quint said as he handed me the reins.

He walked toward the truck where his parents rode. Charlotte was getting Pops's collapsible wheelchair set up.

I rubbed Talin's neck and looked at Jonah. He raised an eyebrow.

"We bonded," I said, in answer to his unspoken question.

"I can tell," he said loosening the belts around Fulton's chest.

I did the same with Talin. She and I followed Jonah and Fulton to the barn.

"We need to take off their saddles and brush them down. Then they can run," Jonah said, slipping the harness from Fulton and removing the bit from his mouth.

I tried to emulate what I saw him do, but I got the harness halfway up and it was stuck.

"Can you help me?" I asked. I stepped back as he walked toward Talin. He removed the harness, and the bit from Talin's mouth. He stroked her gently between the eyes.

"I figured you knew how to do this," he said, walking toward the wall.

"Talin's the first horse I ever rode," I said, watching him hang the harness on a wall hook.

"You seem so at ease. Most people are nervous around horses their first few times," Jonah said, returning to Fulton's side.

"She makes it easy. Anyone would be comfortable around her," I said, shrugging.

"It doesn't work that way," he said, shaking his head. "Talin is a great horse, but she can't make you comfortable around her. It's a partnership. She gives and you give. It's how it works. It's a lot like human relationships in that way," he said, looking at me with that same *trying to figure something out* look he had when we first met.

I felt heat rise to my cheeks. I moved to Talin's side, pretending to be looking at the saddle, hoping he hadn't seen me blush. I didn't know why I had. Yes, he was cute, but lots of guys were. Trent is cute. Had I blushed when he was trying to win me? I couldn't remember. It seemed like a lifetime ago.

"Watch me take Fulton's saddle off. Then you can try and do Talin's," he said as he unbuckled Fulton's saddle. Jonah lifted it and a large blanket from Fulton's back. He carried both into a small room that divided one side of the barn.

I walked to Talin's side, where a large buckle lay against a blanket. I pulled it tight to loosen it. She didn't move. The strap fell loose, swinging in the air. I pulled the saddle off Talin. I strained under its weight and took a step backward. Jonah caught me inches before my butt hit the ground. He lifted me to my feet.

"Here, I can get it," he said, his hands brushing mine as he tried to take the saddle and blanket from me.

"No, I got it. I was just caught off guard. Show me where to put it," I said, trying not to be embarrassed, trying to be indifferent to the closeness of our bodies. I failed in both attempts.

Jonah straightened and turned, walking toward the room. I followed, doing what I could to slow my heart rate.

"This is where Talin's saddle and blanket go," he said, pointing to a small stand next to Fulton's saddle.

I placed Talin's saddle on the stand and said, "This is a nice little room." Once the words were out, I realized how stupid they sounded. I wanted to talk to Jonah, but I had no idea what to say.

"It's called the tack room," he said, picking up two large brushes from a shelf. "Do you want to brush her down?" he asked, handing me a brush.

I took the brush and followed him back to the horses.

I copied what he did.

"How did things go at my grandparents'?" he asked.

"Fine, I guess. Your mom and I were separated from the rest of them, so I don't know what was said. But Nonie and Pops came without a fight," I said, trying to keep my mind in the present.

"They can be tough to persuade at times," he said, shaking his head. "Actually, they can be stubborn to an annoying degree most of the time."

"I got that feeling," I said, watching dust fall from Talin's coat with each brush stroke.

"What were you and my mom doing?" he asked, now brushing Fulton's mane.

"Talking," I said, not willing to say more than that.

Jonah nodded as if he understood that he was not to ask

a follow-up question.

He stopped brushing and patted Fulton.

"You two can go run," he said, looking at them. They each turned and ran in the direction of the stream.

He reached out his hand to me. I hesitated. Did he want to hold my hand?

"Can I have your brush? I'll put it away," he said.

I handed it to him, feeling foolish. He took both brushes to the tack room. I stood, not knowing what to do. I understood now why Sara was constantly trying to be with him. Something about him drew me in.

"I think the food is almost ready. It's been cooking all day," Jonah said, coming out of the tack room and heading to the open barn door.

I walked beside him, growing hungrier by the moment.

"Who's that?" I said, pointing to a man and a dog emerging from the tree line on the west side of the property.

Jonah stiffened. I stopped in my tracks when I recognized the dog.

"It's Mick Jacobson and his dog. Neither is welcome here and both know it," Jonah said, leaving me behind and moving at a swift pace toward them.

East stood from her place at the fire and walked toward Mick. His chin-length black hair looked uneven and knotted. The pistol on his hip reflected the sunlight. Quint walked toward his daughter, his hand resting on the pistol on his belt. Eli followed his dad, and Charlotte held JP and Quinn against her body, where they stood by Nonie and Pops. JP struggled to break free from his mother, but her grip was tight and he soon stopped fighting.

Jonah strode past the fire to join his sister, father, and brother. Sara, Blaise, and Josh stood up, but did not leave their places by the fire. I joined them, standing beside Sara. We looked at one another but did not speak. The tension seemed to encompass the entire property.

Mick and his dog were still fifty yards away, but the dog started forward.

"Call him off," Quint commanded, his pistol aimed at the dog. Quint showed no sign of hesitation.

Mick spat the words, "Wrath, back," while his hand moved to his gun. The dog stopped running. Instead, he paced back and forth at an invisible line, much like he'd done at the no longer existent fence.

"What are you doing here?" Quint said, lowering his pistol only slightly.

"I wanted to check on you and your family. Make sure you were okay. Didn't realize everyone would be here, and some extras. Real colorful group y'all got here," Mick said, looking first at where Nonie and Pops were and then at my friends and me. I could see the smirk on his face, even from where I stood.

Eli said, "You smelled the food. You came to take it. You didn't realize how many of us there would be."

"Thanks for the benefit of the doubt, Father," Mick said. "That's real Christian of you. And nice to see you too, East. Been a long time." A wry smile came across his lips as he eyed her up and down.

Jonah lunged, but East and Eli held him back. Wrath started forward again, and Quint fired a shot at the dog's feet.

"Easy, Quint. You wouldn't want to have to go to confession." Mick laughed.

"Please do not doubt my words," Quint said. He held the pistol firmly in his right hand, no longer aimed at Wrath but at Mick's head. "The next time that dog is within a hundred yards of any member of my family, it will be killed. The same goes for you. Get off my land."

"I was hoping we could put our differences behind us, now that things have changed," Mick said, his sarcastic tone gone.

"Our differences?" Quint's voice shook with anger.

"It's been years. Let it go," Mick said, his tone irritated.

Jonah lunged, and Eli pushed him back. East did not. Quint raised his other hand so that both were holding the pistol aimed at Mick. He said nothing.

"You'll be sorry," Mick said.

"The next time I see you on my property, I will kill you," Quint said, his hatred clear.

Mick laughed before turning and striding back toward the trees. Wrath followed, pivoting every few yards to growl and bare his teeth.

"What was that about?" Sara whispered.

I shook my head, feeling scared and confused.

"I think Quint meant it. I think he will kill that man the next time he sees him," Blaise whispered.

Josh nodded.

* * *

East walked to her mother and took Quinn from her arms. She went inside, her grandmother close behind.

Quint put the gun back between his belt and jeans, his hands shaking as he did so. I couldn't help but wonder if they shook from fear or rage.

"You should have shot him," Jonah said. His eyes continued to watch the trees where Mick and Wrath had disappeared.

"It's not his place to kill," Eli said. "Regardless of how

vile of a human being he is; it is not our decision when he dies."

Jonah's anger shifted to Eli. "You are such a priest. It's like you don't even care what he did."

"You're right. I am a priest and proud of it. But if you think there are not times when I personally want to smash his head in with a shovel, you're wrong. I want him to die and I want him to writhe in pain as he does. But then I catch myself. I—we are called to forgive, if not for his benefit, then for our own. When he dies is not up to me. All human life is sacred. I believe that, not because it is convenient or easy, but because it is what our Lord tells us," Eli answered, his own face red with emotion.

What had this man done? Eli, who was so calm, so filled with peace, hated this man. Hate was something I was sure was against his religion, a religion he was obviously committed to.

Jonah walked away. I did not have the courage to look at him as he passed us on his way to the barn. His anger scared me. If it were up to him, a man would be dead a few yards from where I stood.

Charlotte released JP. He ran out to join his father and his brother. She disappeared into the house. Pops was trying to wheel his chair, but it was stuck in the loose earth. I went to him.

"Can I help you?" I asked.

"It's okay, I don't even know where I'm trying to go. The women don't want me inside. It's best to leave Jonah alone. Eli is calming Quint down. So I'm not sure where to go, but I don't want to sit here," Pops said, sounding as though he doubted his usefulness.

"Can I take you to the fire? My friends and I could use help with the cooking," I said.

"That would be good. Then I could warm up a bit. It's getting colder every day," he said, rubbing his hands together.

"I know," I said, pushing him toward the fire. "That worries me."

"Don't tell my kids, but it worries me too," Pops said.

* * *

Quint went inside, and Eli and JP eventually joined us by the fire.

"Why do we all hate Mick so much?" JP asked.

I felt wrong for being present when that question was asked. It had to do with their family; I had no right to know the answer.

"Because he has done some really bad things," Eli answered, looking at his brother.

"Yes, but why do *we* hate him? What has he done to *us*?" JP asked.

"John Paul," Eli answered, "you must decide for yourself who you hate. No one decides that for you, and I would encourage you not to hate. Hate destroys the person who hates. It is not how God wants us to live." He was watching the flames fight for their freedom before returning to the burning wood.

"You really are a priest," Josh said, almost as if the thought escaped his lips before he realized it.

"I really am," Eli said, his voice lighter.

"So you'll never marry or date or anything?" Sara asked. She seemed genuinely confused by the concept.

"Not if he's sticking to his vows," Pops teased.

"How do you do that?" Josh asked.

"It's my vocation, my calling. At times it can be challenging, but most of the time I experience an overwhelming sense of joy at giving myself freely and completely to God," he said. The joy he spoke of was evident.

Pops looked at me as he spoke. "Eli was called at a young age. He felt his heart stir toward the priesthood when he was eight. The first person he told of his calling was Holt. He encouraged Eli to listen and be open to the possibility that he was being called to the priesthood."

I looked at my friends, not knowing what to say. I was confused. Why would a militant atheist encourage an eight-year-old kid to be a priest?

"Holt? Bria's dad, Holt?" Blaise asked.

Eli and Pops nodded.

"He is my godfather and he was very involved in my early religious formation. He was also my best friend," Eli said with great emotion.

I felt anger rise and tears sting the back of my eyes. How could a man who hated God and felt all people who believed in God were fools have been his godfather? How could this man who never showed any interest in me have been his best friend? Why did my father hate me? Why did he give me nothing of who he actually was? Why did he lie to me time after time? Every word he spoke was a lie.

I stood and walked away. I didn't know where I was going. I saw Talin in the distance and went toward her. When I finally reached her she was standing behind the barn. I flung my arms around her neck, buried my face, and cried. My knees became weak and my grip around her neck tightened. She did not move. She stood strong while I was weak.

"Are you okay?" His voice sounded far away.

Talin nudged me with her head. I let go of her.

Jonah stood beside me. I knew I should feel

embarrassed, but I didn't. I couldn't. My entire life had been a lie. I had no energy left to care what this man thought of me.

"No," I said, biting the inside of my cheeks to keep from crying.

He sat on a bale of hay. "Want to sit down for a minute?" he asked.

His voice sounded different. Had he been crying? I'd never seen a man cry before. I wondered what'd brought Jonah to tears. What had Mick Jacobson done to this family?

I sat on the far end of the straw and leaned my back against the barn. Talin wandered a few feet away and ate some nearby weeds.

"This day sucks," I said.

"Yep," he said.

After some silence, he spoke. "Why has it sucked for you?"

"Everything my father ever told me was a lie."

"That would suck," he said, nodding.

"Thanks," I said sarcastically.

"Well, it would. I remember your dad a little. I was five when you two disappeared. He was a nice guy back then, but it sounds like he changed. I guess losing your wife and son in one day, a day that was supposed to be joyous, can do that to a person." He had leaned against the barn as he spoke.

"My father told me my mom died in a fire. That our house had burned down. It wasn't until your grandmother said something about my brother earlier today, that I remembered how she had really died or that I had a brother," I said, exhausted.

Jonah turned his head to look at me. "I'm sorry. That's not fair to you. It's not fair to change a person's memories," he said.

"Why did he do it?" I asked, feeling the tears start to build.

"I don't know," he said, looking at the ground. "I wish I had answers for you. You deserve answers."

"Thanks," I said, feeling grateful for Jonah's honesty.

"What about you?" I asked.

"Why has this day sucked for me?"

I nodded.

"Evil stood in my backyard," he said, emotion starting to rise in his voice.

"What did he do?" I felt guilty for asking, but I asked not for the pleasure of knowing, but out of a desire to be closer to Jonah and his family, my god-family.

"It's not mine to tell. If it were, I would tell you," he said, looking in my eyes as he spoke.

"Okay," I said, feeling stupid for asking.

"I really would tell you if I could," he said, trying to make me feel better.

I nodded. "Did you tell the police or anything?" I asked. It seemed impossible to me that whatever Mick had done had been legal, not with the amount of hatred everyone felt for him.

Jonah paused as if wondering how much he could divulge. "We did, but then we stopped pursuing prosecution," he said.

"Why?" The question was out before I realized I was asking it.

"It's complicated," he said, and I knew by his tone we were done discussing Mick.

I nodded once. We sat in silence.

"Where were you this morning?" I asked.

"Sleeping," he said.

"Sleeping?" I didn't try to hide the surprise in my voice.

"I volunteered to take the first watch," he said, watching Talin and Fulton drink from the stream.

"What do you mean?" I asked.

He turned his head to look at me. "I stayed up until three, when Eli got up and relieved me. Someone always needs to be awake," he said.

"Were you all afraid of Mick?" I asked, wondering why someone needed to be awake.

"Of Mick or whomever else. It's just good to protect ourselves," he said.

I leaned my head back and watched the horses. Listening to Jonah and Charlotte, it was as if we were in imminent danger—and perhaps we were. I was tired, too tired to feel anything more than confusion.

Jonah leaned forward and propped his arms against his legs. "I'm told you and I were best friends when we were younger. Mom said if we went a day without seeing each other, I cried," he said, looking back at me.

New emotion stirred within me as our eyes met. His were the color of the green sea glass I hunted for every year at summer camp. I turned away and watched Talin and Fulton eating grass near the stream.

He stood, brushing the hay from his jeans. "The others will be wondering where we are," he said.

"You're right," I said, standing and brushing off the hay, happy at the prospect of food, and wishing I had more time alone with Jonah.

Eight

I sat between Sara and Blaise, the three of us in low folding chairs. Josh sat next to Blaise on a log. Jonah sat next to Sara, also on a log. She made sure to sit by him. I could tell she was angry that I'd spent time with him. Sara was one of my best friends, but when she set her sights on a guy she lost sight of everyone else.

East sat next to her brother and Quinn sat between her and her mother. JP sat between his parents and Nonie and Pops sat between their son and oldest grandson. We made an impressive circle around the campfire. I felt safe. I knew the family was bothered by Mick, but I couldn't imagine him trying anything, not when there were so many of us.

"Since this is our Thanksgiving meal, I would like us all to say something we're thankful for," Quint said, taking me off guard.

Every Thanksgiving before this one, I'd spent alone with my father and we never said what we were thankful for.

Charlotte spoke up. "I'll start. I am thankful that *all* of my children," she said, looking at me, "and some of their friends are with us. You go next, John Paul."

"I am thankful my brothers and big sister are here," JP said.

"I am thankful my entire family is together," Quint said, looking first at me and then at his parents.

My mind drifted as the gratitude made its way around the circle. I tried to think of what to say. So many thoughts ran through my mind.

"… and I am thankful I have the most amazing fiancé in the world," Blaise said, giving Josh a hug. No doubt he had said something similar.

It was my turn. I paused for only a moment. "I am thankful for the people who love me." The words brought tears to my eyes. I hadn't realized they would. In the last eighteen years I may have cried half a dozen times, but today … I had spent most of it in tears. It was as if flood gates had been opened and I didn't know how to shut them. I covered my face with my hands. Blaise and Sara both put arms around me.

"I am thankful for my friends new and old," Sara said, holding me while glancing at Jonah.

"I am thankful for the return of an old friend and for new ones," Jonah said, looking at me.

"I am thankful for Quinn," East said.

"Hey, what about me?" JP said, and I laughed out loud, along with everyone else.

"She likes me better. We are sisters," Quinn said, sticking out her tongue at her brother.

I laughed even harder.

"I am thankful for you too, JP," East said, shaking her head.

* * *

The meal was amazing. Quint and Charlotte were excellent cooks. It was a shame they wouldn't have the ingredients to cook many or possibly any more meals like this. There was plenty of food and we ate until the sun started to set. We drank water that East and Quinn had gathered from the stream and then boiled and set aside to cool. There was a little bit of dirt in it, but it mostly settled to the bottom. Even with the dirt the water tasted better than any bottled water.

As the sun set and the wind started to blow, Quinn said, "Momma, I'm cold."

"Okay, Quinny, let's go inside. East, would you come start the fire in the house?" Charlotte said as she stood and led Quinn toward the house. East walked behind them, carrying as many plates as she could.

I shivered and leaned in closer to the fire, its flames being pushed sideways by the wind. With the sun gone and the wind picking up, the temperature was dropping quickly. Silver shadows began to inch toward us. The moon was rising, and by the looks of things it was a full moon.

"This wind isn't good. You know, they predicted a snowstorm for the weekend. The weather guy said it was going to be a brutal winter this year. Said it was going to start early, last long, and be cold throughout," Pops said, holding on to Nonie's hand and leaning toward the fire.

Nonie looked at Pops and said, "If it freezes, everything in the garden will be ruined."

"If we harvest everything now, we won't have any fresh vegetables until the next crop in late spring," Blaise said, concern in her voice.

"I don't think we have a choice. The root vegetables will last for a few months in the cellar, but if the freeze hits them, they will be mush by morning," Nonie said.

"We better get going. It feels like it's dropped ten degrees since Mom took Quinn in," Eli said while standing and stretching.

Quint stood and walked toward his father. "Dad, I'll help get you in. Mom, you need to get in too. No point in having everyone freeze. Jonah, put out the fire. It's too dangerous in this wind," Quint said.

Nonie gathered as many plates as she could carry, and Pops collected the rest on his lap.

Jonah stood and dumped a nearby bucket of water on the fire.

I knew losing the heat of the fire would be painful, but I had no idea how painful. The temperature had gone from seventy degrees when we sat down to dinner, to now probably forty degrees, and dropping every moment.

"Let's get this done so we can get inside," Josh yelled over the wind as he strode to the garden. He and Blaise led the way. The rest of us followed.

At the garden, Blaise took the lead on the harvest. "We have to leave some carrots in the ground so they can go to seed. We'll have to cover them with as many layers as we can. Pile up the dirt around them, like this. Then we'll need to get a blanket for them," she said.

"I'll go get a blanket and tell Mom what we're doing. She may want to come supervise," Eli said, running toward the house.

"Sara and Bria, start picking the rest of the carrots. Don't worry about cleaning them off. We can clean them once we aren't all in danger of freezing. Josh, you and Jonah start digging up the potatoes," Blaise said.

I knelt in the dry earth and began pulling carrots. I had

never gardened before, never pulled a carrot from the earth. It was fun, even in the awful circumstances that surrounded the picking of these carrots. The earth hid the secret of the carrot and not until it was pulled from all it had ever known did I discover its size and shape. Some were long and straight. Others had grown too close together, twisted around each other, both of their growths stunted. Others grew close but had room, their fine, threadlike roots connected to one another, yet the carrots themselves strong and healthy. Their leaves looked silver in the moonlight and the carrots were a variety of colors. I had never seen a carrot any color other than orange, but here I knelt, pulling them from the earth. Some white, some a deep purple, others orange.

Eli returned with Charlotte close behind. Both carried coats and blankets.

"Here, put these on," Charlotte said as she handed everyone their coats. She handed me one that belonged to someone in her family.

One benefit of a large family is you're used to supporting a large family. You have lots of coats, a large garden, a pantry full of food. In my apartment there was maybe a box of crackers and a few yogurts in the fridge.

The coat was much too large for me, but I didn't care. I

zipped it up and pulled the collar around my ears. The wind stopped assaulting my body. It made the harvest far less painful.

"Good idea to save some carrots for seed, Blaise," Charlotte said as she knelt beside her and heaped dirt around the carrots. She then added a worn child's bed quilt on top of the mounds.

I carried a heap of carrots to the back porch. Jonah followed with an armful of potatoes.

"I think the others can handle the garden," he said. "I want to make sure Talin and Fulton are protected from the cold. Do you want to help?" He put the potatoes in a large empty box by the back door.

I placed the carrots on top. "Sure. Let me go tell Sara. I don't want her to think I skipped out on carrot pulling."

"Okay, tell them I went to the barn," he said as he took long strides in that direction.

I ran to the garden.

"Jonah and I are going to make sure the horses are okay. Do you want to come?" I asked Sara. I didn't want her to get mad at me for spending time alone with him.

"No, that's okay. There's a lot to do here. You go. I saw you with Talin earlier. I know she means a lot to you," Sara said, barely stopping her harvesting to speak to me.

"Yeah, she does. I can't explain it. It seems weird," I answered.

"It isn't weird. Some people and some animals have a connection. You and Talin have that. Go check on her. I'll get the carrots done and move on to the potatoes." Sara stood to gather her pile of carrots.

"Okay," I said, before running to the barn.

It was dark in the barn. The moonlight shone through the large openings on either side and the few windows, but the barn was dark anywhere the moonlight did not reach. The barn was silent except for the muted clucking of the chickens.

"Jonah?"

"Over here," he said, his voice panicked.

I walked toward his voice. As I got closer I saw him kneeling on the ground. Talin and Fulton were each lying on their side, next to him. Their noses nearly touched each other. Jonah stroked their necks.

"What is it?" I asked, feeling terror rise inside me. All I knew about horses I had learned today or seen in movies. But I knew enough to know horses shouldn't be lying down like this.

"I don't know. I found them like this. I don't know what's happened." Jonah's voice was small.

"Stay with them, Bria. I have to get my dad. He's a

vet." Jonah sprinted from the barn.

I took his place kneeling between the horses, stroking their necks. Their breathing was shallow and quick. I looked in Talin's eye. It was out of focus and glazed over.

A few moments later Jonah returned, with Quint running behind him.

He knelt beside them. He placed his ear near their mouths and listened for their breath. "I need more light. You two get a fire started, and get blankets on these horses. They are ice cold," he said.

"I don't want to leave her," I said quietly as I stroked her.

"What she needs from you now is the fire I asked for and a blanket," Quint said, commanding me to action.

"Come on," Jonah said, taking my hand and pulling me up and out of the way.

He ran to the tack room, returning in an instant with two blankets.

He threw me one of them. "Put this on Talin."

I laid it gently over her, kissed her head, and followed Jonah out of the barn. The wind hit me hard, driving me sideways into the barn wall.

"You okay?" he yelled over the howling wind.

"Yes," I called, trying hard to stay on my feet. I kept my eyes on Jonah, the wind causing even his large frame to swerve now and then.

We reached the wood pile and he handed me a few small logs, before turning to run back to the barn with his arms full. I followed as fast as I could.

He threw the wood down and grabbed a rake. He cleared the straw away from an area in the center of the barn, not far from the stall Talin and Fulton were in. As the rake lifted the straw the wind blew it on its way through the barn.

He knelt, gathering a small clump of straw and carefully stacking wood around it to make a teepee shape. He dug in his pocket and retrieved a lighter. The straw caught instantly and the wood ignited soon after.

"Get that door closed," Jonah commanded.

As he ran to the back door, I ran to the front and pulled it shut. The wind blew hard and the door shook, but did not slide open.

Jonah ran around pulling the wooden windows closed.

The doors and windows rattled, but inside, the barn was still and dark. Moonlight seeped in at every tiny opening. Even so, the fire was now our only substantial source of light.

I watched Quint use his stethoscope. He listened to Fulton's massive chest and then moved to Talin. He pulled up her eyelid and peered into her eye.

"Their pupils are dilated," he said, more to himself than to us.

A moment later he was up and running.

"I'll be back," he said as he ran to the barn door, slid it open a few inches, and disappeared into the night.

I knelt by Talin and petted her. Jonah sat with his back against the barn wall, his hand on Fulton's head. His mouth moved but no words came out.

"What are you doing?" I asked.

"Praying," he answered.

The barn door slid open again.

"What happened?"

Sara's voice surprised me. I expected to hear Quint's voice. Charlotte, Blaise, Josh, and Eli entered with her. They lined the outside of the stall.

I shook my head and bit my lip. I turned away from my friends. I couldn't look at them without feeling the hurt more intensely.

Charlotte came into the stall and knelt down beside me. She placed one hand on my back and the other on Fulton. Eli stood on the edge of the small stall. He pulled the beads from his pocket and began to say words that seemed vaguely familiar to me. I wondered if I had heard my mother say them. Jonah said the words with Eli and so did Charlotte. I turned when I heard Blaise's voice join in the chorus of "Hail Mary, full of grace, the Lord is with Thee …." I didn't understand the meaning of the words, but their methodical repetition was soothing.

The words stopped when Quint rushed back into the stall. I moved to the other side of Talin, careful to keep my hand on her. I wanted her to know I was there. That I believed in her. That she was going to be okay.

"What is it?" Charlotte said as she stood to make room.

Quint took her spot and emptied a grocery bag: out came water bottles, huge syringes, and a black powder.

"Poison. It has to be. There's nothing else that could come on this fast and strong and hit them both at the same time," Quint said as he twisted open the top of a water bottle.

"Poison?" Eli and Charlotte said in unison.

I looked at Jonah. The muscle in his jaw tightened.

"Has to be," Quint said as he poured black powder into the syringes.

"The stream?" Charlotte said.

Quint nodded.

"But we drank water from the stream at dinner," Josh said.

Quint said, "When I was inside, I asked East when she gathered that water. She said earlier in the day, before we got back from Mom and Dad's. Before—" Quint stopped.

"Before Mick," Jonah said. I could hear the hatred in his words.

Quint nodded.

Jonah's fist tightened. He wanted to kill him. I know he did. I wanted the same thing.

"I'm giving them activated charcoal," Quint said as he opened Talin's mouth, pushing the syringe in as far as he could before emptying the contents down her throat.

"Will that work?" I asked, my voice shaking out of fear and hatred.

"I don't know," he said. He emptied the second syringe into Fulton's mouth. "But it's all I can do. That, and pray." He sat back on his feet, petting both horses gently on their necks.

Nine

Eli lugged more wood into the barn. My friends carried in what was left of the uncontaminated water. Charlotte brought out as many quilts and blankets as could be spared. Jonah and I covered Talin and Fulton with four blankets each, leaving one for each of us. The wind pushed violently against the barn and the snow fell.

Quint showed Jonah and me how to mix the activated charcoal with the bottled water and administer it to Talin and Fulton.

"You have to do this every four hours. In two hours give them each a syringe of water, then do that every four hours. Here, take my watch," Quint said, handing it to Jonah.

As Jonah fastened it to his wrist, I saw the small crown, the symbol for Rolex. That explained why it still worked. It ran on movement, not a battery.

"Come get me if anything changes," Quint said.

Jonah nodded.

"Walk me out, Jonah," he said as he stood. Jonah matched his father's stride to the front of the barn.

Quint kept his voice low. Though I couldn't hear what he said, I watched Quint hand Jonah his pistol.

Quint zipped up his coat. Pulled on his sock hat. Gave his son a hug. Slid the large barn door open enough to slip through. Jonah pulled the door closed a little more and watched through a small crack as his father walked to the house. The wind pushed in through the small opening and snow gathered around Jonah's feet.

He shut the door, latching it against the wind and the night.

Jonah stopped on his way back to his spot against the wall, to place another log on the fire. It burned brightly. Our only source of light. Our only source of heat. It was enough to keep us from freezing, but not much more. The barn had no insulation and the wind pushed the cold air through every small crack. When the wind blew its hardest, the fire was pressed to the ground. There were lots of small cracks. We sat on a thick layer of straw, bundled in our coats and blankets. The night would not be spent in comfort.

My friends wanted to sleep in the barn with us. Charlotte said no. Eli also offered. Charlotte said no. She said she would not allow more than two of us to freeze to death and she knew she couldn't stop Jonah and she doubted she could stop me.

I don't know how I bonded so quickly with Talin, but I had. There was something about her. The thought of her hurting made my stomach turn. The thought of her dying was unimaginable. I pushed the thought from my mind and stared at the fire.

"You should try and sleep," Jonah said. "I'll take the first four hours. You can take the next four."

"Thanks, but I'm not planning to sleep tonight," I said. I pulled part of a blanket up over the back of my head so only my face was exposed to the cold air.

Jonah pulled his blanket behind him, crossed his legs, and leaned forward on his elbows. The space was so small that when he did this his head was over Fulton's neck. My legs were also crossed and my knees touched Talin's ears. Part of me wanted to lean against her so she could feel me and to offer her warmth, but I was afraid to touch her. Afraid it would hurt her in some way.

"Okay," he said, his eyes going from Fulton to Talin. He picked up the gun, clicked something on it, and laid it on the ground next to him.

"Why did your dad give you the gun?" I asked.

"To protect you," he said, his eyes not leaving the horses.

"Protect me?" I asked, confused.

Jonah nodded.

"From who?" I asked, though I already knew.

"From Mick or anyone that might be with him, if he or they come here tonight. He said to do whatever it took to keep you safe."

"Why would Mick try and hurt me?"

"Why did he poison Talin and Fulton? He's evil," Jonah said.

"I don't believe in evil," I said, not knowing what else to say. I knew the world had changed, but this felt unreal.

He turned to look at me. "You can believe in evil or not believe in evil. That doesn't alter its existence."

"Your saying it exists doesn't automatically mean it exists," I said, knowing that a theory that could not be disproved was a logical fallacy.

"Have you never felt it within yourself? Never sensed it in others?" he asked.

I said nothing. I shivered partly from the cold and partly from the realization that as long as Mick Jacobson was near, we weren't safe.

The wind rattled the windows, and for a moment I imagined someone trying to come in. I glanced at Jonah.

"It's okay. He won't try anything tonight. This is a bad storm and it's getting worse by the minute. That will work to our advantage—if we don't freeze to death," he said, pulling the blanket tightly around his shoulders.

His eyes turned from Fulton and Talin to the fire. I watched him for longer than I meant to. I remembered then where I was and what this day had been. I followed his gaze and stared at the fire he had created to warm us and give us light. The fire that kept the darkness at bay. The fire that would keep our blood from freezing in our veins.

This had been one of the worst days of my life. The day my mother and brother died was far worse, but today was the day those memories flooded my mind. In some ways, to me at least, they died again today. The memories had been shoved so deep inside, that I had forgotten. Forgotten I had a brother. Forgotten how my mother died. Both of those facts mattered.

Today was the day I realized my father had lied to me about everything of importance. The existence of my brother, the death of my mother, the faith she shared with him. They had not been atheists, as he had said. She had not wanted me raised as an atheist. She had loved God and so had he. And yet now …. How deeply he must hate the God whose existence he denies. There was no other way to explain the lies. Perhaps he thought he was protecting me or perhaps the hatred consumed him. Either way, the result was I didn't know who my mother was, or my father, for that matter. I didn't know where I came from or anything about the faith I was brought into as an infant.

"You okay?" Jonah asked.

I blinked and looked into his green eyes. "I was thinking about my dad," I said.

"What about him?" Jonah asked, leaning his head against the wall, his eyes looking at my own.

I blinked again. His presence made me uncomfortable, yet I longed to be closer to him.

"The lies," I said, shaking my head.

Jonah nodded knowingly, hunching his torso forward. "Did he tell you your mom loved you?"

"Yes."

"Then he didn't lie to you about *everything*."

I looked down.

Jonah said, "I can't imagine how hard losing your mom and brother was for him. I can't imagine how angry he was at God. I would hope I would have a strong enough faith to not hate God, but it would be hard." He leaned his head back against the barn wall.

"He should have been honest, that's all. Let me make up my own mind about things," I said, not willing to let the anger go so easily.

"Have you always been honest with him?" he asked.

I lowered my gaze. "This isn't about my actions or my honesty, it's about his," I said, angry at Jonah for defending my father.

"Your dad is human. He makes mistakes. We all make

mistakes. If your dad asked for forgiveness from God, he would be given that forgiveness. I think you owe him the same," Jonah said, turning to look at me.

"You have no idea what I've been through. No idea of the consequences of his lies," I said, my anger mixing with sadness.

"You're right," he said, nodding his head slowly.

I said nothing. I was angry at Jonah, at my father, but most of all at myself.

"If it helps, I'm sorry for whatever you've gone through," he said.

"Me too," I said, leaning my head against the wall. I fought back tears, afraid they would freeze on my face.

* * *

I sat staring at nothing. Not awake, not asleep. Somewhere in between. I thought of my mother and my father. The anger I felt for him lessened, though at times still overwhelmed me.

Jonah sat up and filled a syringe with water. He opened Fulton's mouth and forced it as far to the back as he could. He filled it again and did the same with Talin.

"Do you think they will live?" I asked.

"I don't know," he whispered, stroking Talin's neck.

Jonah stood and walked to the fire. The fire brightened

when he moved the burning wood and placed two more large logs onto it. I watched him in the firelight. He was strong and sure of himself ... two things I had never been.

He came back to the small open space next to Fulton and sat down, careful not to step on him. Once he was back in his spot he pulled his blanket around his shoulders.

He glanced in my direction before turning to watch the fire.

I watched the flames dance in the night air. The wind had diminished. The night was quiet.

"Bria, can I ask you something?" Jonah said without turning in my direction.

"I guess so," I said, too tired to care one way or the other.

"When we were walking here I heard you say something about a guy. Do you miss him?" he said, turning to look at me.

I paused, wondering why Jonah was asking about Trent. "Yes, I do."

Jonah nodded, but said nothing.

"Why do you ask?" I said, turning to face him.

"I don't know. I could tell your friends don't like him, or don't like him with you. I guess I was curious," he said, looking at me as he spoke.

I exhaled audibly. "No, my friends don't like him and

he doesn't like them. He and I were … we were together a long time. We had our ups and downs and at times things between us were a little … intense," I said, looking at the fire, not wanting to make eye contact.

Jonah sat looking at me. I pretended not to notice and kept my gaze on the flames. After several minutes of him staring at me, I turned to look at him.

"Did he ever hit you?"

I could sense anger and sadness disguised within his calm tone.

"No," I lied.

He looked in my eyes. "You're lying," he said in a sympathetic whisper.

How did he know? How could he possibly know? I turned my head to face the fire.

"Why would I lie?" I asked.

"I don't know, but you should figure that out," he said, still looking at the side of my face.

I said nothing. He turned his face to the fire. I thought about his words. They weren't meant to upset me. I knew that. Jonah's heart was good and kind. He was like Josh in that way. But why did he care?

He was right, though. I did need to figure it out. I will probably never see Trent again and yet he has control over me. Still, I feel ashamed of what he did to me, of how he treated me. But no, I am not ashamed of him hitting me; I'm ashamed that after he hit me, I stayed.

Jonah didn't know my past; he didn't know I deserved nothing more than what Trent offered. Jonah's gaze and his questions told me he thought I deserved better, but would he still have those thoughts if he knew all I had done?

No. I knew he would not.

Ten

"Bria, wake up."

I opened my eyes. The sunlight filtered through the cracks in the side of the barn. The fire still burned, but its appearance was not as bright. The air was not warm, but at least it wasn't any colder.

"I think they are going to be okay," Jonah said, almost laughing as he said the words.

Talin and Fulton both lay on their stomachs. Talin turned her head. Her large brown eyes met my eyes, and I leaped forward, throwing my arms around her neck. She laid her head gently on my back.

"Their breathing started to improve around four, but they each just moved a second ago," Jonah said as he petted them in turn.

"I fell asleep. I'm sorry. I meant to stay awake and help you," I said.

"You had a rough day yesterday. You needed to sleep." He was looking at me in a weird way.

I ran my fingers through my hair. Still he looked at me.

"What?" I asked, feeling like there must be something on my face or stuck in my hair.

"What were you dreaming about?" he asked, smirking.

"I don't remember. Why?"

"You said my name a few times in your sleep," he said, unsuccessfully suppressing a grin.

My face colored. "About Talin and Fulton. I wanted you to help them," I said, hoping he believed me.

He nodded and the grin faded. "I'm going to go get Dad so he can check them out," he said, standing and stretching.

Jonah ran to the barn door, his coat zipped tightly around his chest. He unlatched the door and slid it open. He was met with a wall of snow half his size. I stood, wrapping blankets around me as I walked toward him ... while wishing for heat, needing a shower, craving a chai tea. When I stood beside him, the snow came up to my hips.

"What are you going to do?" I asked.

"It's not as high in the yard. This is a drift," he said.

He ran to the tack room and returned with a shovel.

Within a few minutes he had a path through the snowdrift. The snow in the rest of the yard didn't reach above the top of his boots. I watched as he ran to the back door of the house and knocked loudly.

A few moments later he and his dad were walking toward me.

"How are they doing?" Quint asked, looking at me as he entered the barn.

"Much better, thanks to Jonah," I said as we went to the horses.

Quint knelt beside Talin and Fulton. He listened to their hearts and their breathing. He positioned their heads so light hit their eyes and he could see their pupils.

"I think they are out of danger. Get them some feed and gather snow for them to drink. Hopefully, in a few days they will be back to normal," he said, standing and petting Talin between the ears. He bent down and picked up the pistol Jonah had left in the hay. He slid it between his belt and his jeans.

"How did you two do last night?" he asked, turning his attention to us, raising an eyebrow at Jonah.

Heat rose to my cheeks. I answered, "I fell asleep almost as soon as you left. It was Jonah who took care of Talin and Fulton."

"Good job, son," he said, suppressing a smile.

"I just did what you said to do," Jonah said with a hint of irritation in his voice.

Feeling embarrassed and wanting to get away from both of them, I said, "I'm going to gather some snow. Do you have a bucket I can use?"

"There's one in the tack room," Jonah said, his voice kind but distant.

* * *

Outside, I did my best to step where Jonah and Quint had stepped. My sneakers could not keep the snow out. I carefully brushed clean snow into the bucket. I thought about Jonah's tone of voice. His dad was clearly asking if anything had happened between Jonah and me. I found it embarrassing, but Jonah found it insulting. It made him angry. I knew he was out of my league and I wasn't good enough for him, but it hurt to realize he must be thinking the same thing.

I walked into the barn carrying the bucket full of snow. Jonah and his dad were having an intense discussion that stopped as soon as I entered. I pretended not to notice. I dumped the snow into the trough.

"I'm going to get some more," I said, and walked back outside, my heart racing in anger.

Sara came toward me. "How are the horses?" She had a scarf wrapped around the top of her head and neck. Her coat was zipped up to her chin.

"They are going to be okay," I said through gritted teeth.

"Then why are you mad?" she asked, cocking her head to watch me.

"No, I'm not. I'm just tired. It was a long night," I lied.

"Bria, I know your angry voice and your tired voice. This is your angry voice," she said, reaching down to help scoop snow into the bucket.

"It's totally stupid. I'll tell you later, okay?" I tried to sound not angry. "Will you take this into the barn and dump it into the trough? I need to warm up."

"Yeah, okay, if you're sure you're all right," she said, taking the bucket from me.

"I'm fine. Nothing a hot shower wouldn't cure," I said.

"Don't remind me. I haven't bathed in three days," she said.

"None of us have," I said as I started to walk to the house.

"I know, it's gross," she called after me.

* * *

Inside, blankets and pillows were spread all over the floor and the couches. Quinn was still asleep on the floor, close to the fireplace. The rest of the family was nowhere to be seen. The heat from the fire felt good. I slipped off the heavy coat and sat in front of the heat, watching Quinn sleep.

Josh and Blaise came into the room. I stood and walked toward them so we wouldn't wake Quinn. I sat at the kitchen table.

"You look awful," Josh said, sitting beside me.

"Josh, that was mean," Blaise said, sitting on my other side.

"It's okay. Where's everyone else?" I said. I didn't care how I looked. I was tired, hungry, cold, and I wanted to go home.

"They are having a church service in Charlotte and Quint's room," Blaise answered.

"A church service?" I asked.

"Yeah," Josh answered. "Eli's a priest, you know. So he's doing their Mass."

"I know, but it's weird they are having a church service in their house," I said.

"It's not like they can drive to church," Blaise said.

"I guess," I said, slipping the coat back on. I wanted to sit in front of the fire, but didn't want to wake Quinn.

Blaise looked at me. "How are Talin and Fulton? Jonah ran in here and said they were doing better. But your face says otherwise," she asked.

"They are doing better. Jonah did a great job taking care of them. Quint thinks they will be back to normal in a few days," I said, pulling the coat around me, crossing my arms in the process.

"So, why do you look like this?" Josh said, gesturing to my face.

"Like what?" I demanded. Josh's words were too much.

"Like nothing. You look fine. We are all having a hard time," Blaise said, petting my arm.

I pulled myself away from her touch. "I'm not having a hard time," I said, my voice cracking. I stood and walked away.

I needed to be by myself. I needed to take a shower, to change my clothes, I needed things to be back to normal. I wanted to go outside, but it was freezing. I went upstairs.

There was boiled water in the bathroom. I looked in the mirror. I had dirt on my face and straw in my hair. No wonder Jonah was repulsed by the idea of me. I rinsed my face. The chill of the water was like a shock going through my body.

I went to JP's room and found my hairbrush. I brushed my hair and pulled it back in a ponytail. The oil didn't show when it was pulled back, or at least that's what I told myself. I found clean clothes and took them with me into the bathroom. I took the bucket of freezing boiled water into the bathtub, took a deep breath, and washed myself as quickly as possible.

I put on my clean clothes.

Back in JP's room, I was still freezing. I looked through my suitcase for warmer clothes. I shook my head when I pulled out my bikini. How I wished for a sweater, but I had none.

"Planning on going swimming?" East asked, amused. She held a sleepy Quinn in her arms.

"No, I was looking for something warm to put on, but I don't have anything," I answered.

"Come with me. I have some things you can wear."

We entered the room she and Quinn shared when she was home from college. It was decorated for Quinn, with a purple rug and butterflies stuck to the wall. A toddler bed covered by a purple-and-pink flowered quilt was against one wall and a twin bed against the other wall. It had no quilt or pillow, only gray sheets. She sat Quinn down on the small bed. Quinn immediately buried herself under her quilt. East knelt before the twin bed and pulled a plastic storage bin out.

"Quinn has taken the entire closet and most of the dresser space in here. All of my things are in these," she said, popping the lid open.

"Does it bother you? Losing all your space to your

sister?" I asked. I knew several friends from college who were upset when their childhood room was turned into something else.

"Why would it bother me? I'm eighteen. It's right that she should have this space as her own," East said as she rummaged through the plastic bin.

"Here, you can wear this," she said, handing me a sweatshirt that read, SAINT JOHN SEMINARY.

"Thanks," I said, pulling it on. "Where's it from?"

"It's the seminary where Eli went and Jonah goes—or went, before all of this happened," East said, pulling out more clothes from the bin.

"What's a seminary?" I asked.

"It's sort of like a school that trains priests. I mean it's more than that, but that's the main point of it, I guess." She closed the bin and slid it back under her bed.

Trying to hide the shock in my voice, I said, "Jonah's going to be a priest?"

"That's his plan, or was his plan. I don't know now." She sat on the floor. "He hadn't told you?" she asked, looking up at me.

I shook my head. "Why would he?" I said, hoping she couldn't hear the hurt in my voice.

"It seemed like you two were spending a decent amount of time together. I thought you might talk about things," she said.

"We really haven't talked about much more than Talin and Fulton," I said, chewing on my lip.

Quinn sat up in bed. "Can I get dressed now?" she asked, sounding irritated.

"Yeah, sure, pick out something warm," East said. She stood and picked up the pile of clothes.

"Here, you and Blaise and Sara can wear these if you want to," she said, handing me the clothes. I reached for them.

"I'm sorry he didn't tell you. He can be so stupid sometimes," she said, letting go of the pile.

"What? No, he had no reason to tell me. Thanks for the clothes. Blaise and Sara thank you too," I said, forcing a smile.

* * *

Back in JP's quiet room I sat on his bed and stared out the large window. The world was white and it looked beautiful. There was ice on the inside of the window. I shivered and pulled a pair of East's jeans over my yoga pants. I rolled up the cuffs and thought of Jonah. He owed me nothing. He had no obligation to tell me anything about himself or his life, but still I felt hurt that he hadn't told me he was going to be a priest. I knew nothing about religion or the specific types of religions, but I did know Catholic priests didn't marry or date. His not telling me confirmed how little I meant to him. No wonder he was mad at his dad for asking about us. Not only did he find me repulsive, but he was also going to be a priest.

I heard footsteps behind me. "There you are," Sara said from the doorway.

I turned to face her.

"What are you doing up here?" she asked, coming to sit next to me.

"I wanted to try and get cleaned up," I said.

"Where'd you get the sweatshirt?" she asked.

"From East. She was bringing Quinn up to get dressed and she said I could wear it. Here, she gave me these for the three of us," I said, handing her the stack of clothes.

"Awesome! I'm freezing," she said, digging through the clothes and pulling out a plain gray sweatshirt. She took off her coat and pulled it on over her thin sweater.

We sat in silence for a moment, each of us staring out the window. Our breath froze as it left our lips.

"Are you worried about your dad or Trent?" she asked. I could hear the worry in her voice.

"I try not to think about them," I answered. "What about you? You worried about your mom and sister?"

Sara nodded, and sudden tears spilled. I pulled her to me and held her while she cried.

Eleven

The days passed hard and slow. Things that once had taken minutes now consumed hours. The primary focus of every day was securing enough food and water, and not freezing.

The snow melted after only two days. We gathered as much as we could the first day, when it was clean and fluffy. We filled everything we could. The stream was no longer an option for us or the horses. We never knew when Mick would try and poison us again. We did use it for washing our clothes. Though it was so cold my hands turned numb before I finished washing even one pair of underwear.

The diagram Quint had been drawing on the legal pad the first day I met him was for a meat smoker. Smoking meat was the only way we had of preserving it. Everyone worked with him to build it; even Quinn and JP contributed in their own ways. Once it was finished we began smoking the meat, first from Charlotte's freezer and then from Nonie's. Each batch took two days of almost constant attention to ensure the fire was smoking the right amount. Two good-sized batches were completed. We were fortunate—the freezing temperatures bought us time and kept the meat from spoiling.

At every meal we ate some kind of meat and whatever vegetable was most likely to go bad first. We saved items from the pantry as a last option. We always had enough food to survive, though never enough to feel satisfied. Charlotte and Quint ate the least of any of us. They would take their allotted servings but would never eat it all, always saving some for JP and Quinn.

It had been only a week since the light, but already our bodies were changing. The softness was gradually leaving, replaced by harder muscle. Faces were slimming, adhering more closely to the bone structure beneath the skin. All of the men had beards in various stages of growth. The hair on my own legs had gone beyond the initial cactus stage and was now soft. Before the light I would have thought this gross; now I was happy for the small amount of insulation it offered.

When I wasn't working I was keeping an eye on Talin and Fulton, shepherding them away from the stream if they ventured near it. We all took turns doing this, but Jonah and I spent the most time watching over them.

I did my best to avoid Jonah. I was polite when he was near, but tried not to look into his eyes or notice how sweet his smile was beneath his light brown beard. When all else was done and he was watching the horses, I sat by the fire in the house, trying to stay warm. The days were tolerable, but the nights were brutal. The temperature was often below freezing. The Pages' house was modern, with an open floor plan and high ceilings. Their fireplace put out some heat, but not enough to overpower the blanket of cold that engulfed every room.

* * *

We sat around the kitchen table eating dinner. Josh and Blaise volunteered to watch the horses while they grazed, to allow both Jonah and me to eat in the house—a rarity.

Pops put his fork on his plate that had contained a small piece of grilled steak and half a potato. He looked around the table. "We can't stay here," he said.

"What?" Charlotte said, looking up at him.

"We can't stay here," Pops repeated.

"I think she wanted you to explain what you meant, not just say the words again," Nonie said from her place between Charlotte and Pops.

"We haven't got water; this house is too darn cold. We

have a lunatic next door. We need to leave," Pops said, leaning back in his wheelchair.

Quint looked at his father. "Where would we go, Dad? Your house?"

Pops shook his head. "No, our house would be no better," he said.

"Then where?" Quint asked, confused.

Pops looked at me. "Bria's house," he said.

I choked on a bite of potato. Sara hit me on the back. Harder than she needed to.

"Oww," I said, looking at her and twisting my back to make it feel better.

"Sorry," she said, "I forgot how strong I am now."

Jonah laughed, though his eyes remained focused on the two small bits of food he had left on his plate.

All other eyes were on me. I shifted and tried to ignore the stares.

I looked at Pops. "What do you mean, my house?"

"I mean your house. Or your grandparents' house, to be more accurate," Pops said.

"My grandparents' house?" I asked.

Quint leaned back in his chair, looking at his father as if something was becoming clear to him. "I'd forgotten about that house," he said.

"Your father and I had too, until this morning," Nonie said, looking at Quint and nodding.

Pops turned his attention back to me. "There are two houses on your family's property. The one you lived in which is newer and small, and the much much older one. It never had electricity. It was built different. The walls are stone, there are fireplaces in almost every room, the kitchen fireplace has an oven built into it, the way it was done two centuries ago. And it is upstream from Mick. He would have to find a different way to kill us," Pops said, seemingly unfazed by the thought of someone trying to kill him and his family.

"There's no way it's still standing. And if it is, there's no way it's safe for us to go in, let alone live in it," Quint said, shaking his head.

"When that house was built, it was meant to last generation after generation. No doubt it will have decades' worth of dust and probably a few critters we would need to kick out or eat, but we wouldn't freeze like we're doing now. Not to mention the thousand acres that it sits on. We could hunt and cut down trees as we needed," he said.

"A thousand acres?" I said, staring at him.

"That's how much your family owns. The largest in the county, probably the largest in the state," Pops answered.

"Wow, Bri, I had no idea," Sara said.

"Neither did I," I said.

"What about Talin and Fulton?" Jonah asked.

"We'd take them, of course. That's how we'd get there," Pops answered.

"I remember an old barn. I'd be shocked if it was still standing, but it might be," Quint said.

"What if the house and barn, what if all of it is gone, fallen down or uninhabitable?" Eli asked.

"Then we could either come back or stay at Esther and Holt's house," Nonie said.

I flinched at the mention of my parents. I hadn't thought of it as their house. I forgot for a moment all the memories it would hold.

"At least we would still be upstream, have the land to hunt. The house is smaller than this one, so it would be easier to heat," Pops added.

"What about our home?" Charlotte said.

"If things change, we could come back," Nonie said, trying to sound hopeful.

"If Mick hasn't burned it to the ground," Jonah said under his breath, yet loud enough for all to hear.

"This is our home. This is where our children were raised," Quint said, his arm around Charlotte.

"Yes," Pops said, "and it's where they will freeze to death or die of poisoning if we don't leave. The snow and cold has kept Mick away, but it's only a matter of time until he gets on a rampage of some sort and heads our way. And we aren't hard for him to get to, being right next door. At least there we'd have thirty miles between us, and stone walls to protect us."

I watched as JP leaned on his elbows, slowly eating his beef. The hard work and freezing temperatures had taken its toll on him too. The gregariousness that had defined him when we met was gone. He was subdued, still happy much of the time, but the exuberance and joy were gone.

"Pops is right. We have to leave," I said, looking at Quint and Charlotte.

Jonah lifted his head and looked at me. I pretended not to notice. Eli watched his brother watch me.

"I don't think we should make a rash decision," Charlotte cautioned.

Careful not to look at me as he spoke, Jonah said, "Bria's right. We have to go. We can't stay here. Not with Mick next door."

"What do you think, Mom?" Quint asked, looking at Nonie.

She paused and looked at Charlotte. "I know what it means to leave your home, to leave this home. This is where Pops and I raised Quint, where I have watched my grandkids grow. I want them to continue to grow, to continue to live. We all know Mick has caused our family immense sorrow, but out of that sorrow something good was brought forth. However, I think the next hurt he causes us will lead to death—his or ours, and neither is acceptable. The next time we meet him someone will die. I feel it deep within me. I do not want that to happen. None of us at this table wants that to happen." She glanced at each of us and then at Charlotte, who sat beside her. "I agree with Jonah and Bria—we must leave our home," she said, taking Charlotte's hand in her own.

Charlotte wiped a tear from her eye but said nothing.

Sara asked, "How will we get to Bria's? Don't we have to go right by his property?"

"If we're all together and enough of us are armed, he won't try anything," Jonah said, looking at Sara.

"Then he would know we were no longer here," Charlotte said, her voice cracking. "He would destroy our home. We could never return."

No one spoke. She was right. I hated the thought of that man in their home. These people who were so good, so kind. They did not deserve their home destroyed, their collective treasures stolen or disgraced.

"We don't need to make this decision tonight," Nonie said, still holding Charlotte's hand.

Pops spoke, "I disagree. We do need to make this

decision tonight. We have a lot of people here, not to mention two horses and a handful of chickens. We require a lot of water. What we have won't last but another day or two."

"Is there no way to drink the water from the stream?" Charlotte said, looking at Quint. "What if we boiled it longer?"

Quint shook his head. "Boiling it will kill bacteria but won't necessarily get rid of poison like he used on Fulton and Talin. That was probably some sort of heavy metal, battery acid, antifreeze, the list goes on. And even if we could boil all of that out, we can't keep the animals out of it forever, and we can't keep taking turns sleeping in the barn to protect them. That isn't safe," he said, looking at his wife and apologizing with his eyes.

"Excuse me," Charlotte said fleeing from the table. Escaping into her room.

We sat in silence, each of us eating the few morsels remaining on our plate.

* * *

That night, as every night, we slept on the family room floor. Nonie and Pops each had a couch. Charlotte and Quinn shared the recliner. JP slept between his father and oldest brother. Josh volunteered to sleep with Jonah in the barn. They would sleep lying as close to the fire as possible without catching themselves on the fire. The horses would sleep nearby. The doors would be latched and the pistol would be within Jonah's reach. East, Blaise, Sara, and I filled in the rest of the floor. The room wasn't overly large; its floor was completely covered in sheets and blankets.

The floor was hard, the fire warm. The bedrooms, with their soft mattresses, were out of the question. Quint had an old mercury thermometer which he took up to JP's room. It got as high as 50°F during one sunny day, but it was often 36° or lower at night.

Pops was right; we couldn't stay here. Not if we had another choice, a choice that was created for the world we now lived in. A world without electricity, without machines, without heat.

Twelve

A week and a day after we arrived at the Page home, we walked away from it.

Silent tears slipped down Charlotte's face as we loaded everything we could into her full-size van. It was packed from floor to ceiling, every inch full of clothes, blankets, what food we had left, tools, Quint's veterinary supplies, books, and family treasures that Charlotte could not leave. We'd gone through all of the water and much of the food brought from Pops and Nonie's home. Even on a rationed diet we were going through our resources way too fast. We needed to hunt and we needed fresh water. It took a day for Charlotte and Quint to agree on what to bring and what to leave. We all helped pack the van. Eli and Sara were in charge of stacking and organizing to get everything in. They said it was like a life-sized version of Tetris.

East made a plea to go into town to check on the people who had once been part of their lives. Quint and Charlotte had sympathized with her, but in the end said it was too dangerous. By now, people from the larger cities had probably made their way into their small town looking for resources. People were hungry, thirsty, desperate. No, we would not go into town. Not because they did not care about these people, but because Quint and Charlotte were determined to keep their family alive and together.

Now with every step we took we got closer to the home I had once shared with my parents. I pushed the memories down, not allowing them to surface.

Pops, Nonie, and Quinn rode inside of the van pulled by Fulton and Talin. A large shotgun sat between Pops and the driver's side door. I held Talin's reins and Jonah held Fulton's. We each carried packs on our backs and Jonah carried a broken shovel. The metal snapped at the base of the wood, when Jonah tried to dig in the frozen earth. The result was a perfect spear.

He and I said nothing as we walked. We'd spent little time together since the night in the barn and no time alone except in passing. It seemed neither one of us wanted to be alone with the other. It was better that way. Easier.

The rest of the family flanked the van on either side. The chickens were in a small cage on top of the van, covered with blankets to help ease their nerves. We needed them to lay eggs and they wouldn't do that if they were totally stressed. At least that's what Nonie said.

Quint led our caravan, the pistol at his side and a duffel

bag on his back. Behind me walked Josh and Blaise, Quint's hunting rifle slung across her shoulders. Her dad had taught her how to shoot when she was younger. It turned out she was really good. Josh carried a large pack on his back, with the few items he and Blaise possessed.

Sara walked closely behind Jonah. She'd noticed the lack of contact between Jonah and me, and had increased the attention she showed him. She knew he was going to be a priest; I'd told her the day East told me, but she didn't care. I wished I didn't.

Charlotte and JP walked behind Sara. JP carried a small backpack full of the few toys and books he had been allowed to bring with us. His mom carried a small bag on her back and a rifle in her hands. She, too, was a good shot. Though not as good as Blaise.

Eli and East followed behind the van. Eli, because he refused to carry a gun despite the command of his father, carried an ax. I respected his beliefs that it was wrong to kill, though I had to think that I would prefer to be shot to death than chopped to death. East, like her mother, carried a gun, one of her grandfather's. All were loaded, ready to defend us if necessary.

The trek to my parents' house would take close to fifteen hours. We left at first light. Quinn had been carried, sleeping, to the van and laid on her grandmother's lap. She was wrapped tightly in blankets. Still, she moaned when she felt the freezing wind brush her face.

Unlike at Thanksgiving, the moon was now almost nonexistent. We would not be able to walk far in the dark; it would not be possible. We had less than twelve hours of daylight. I was scared, though I would never admit it. I didn't know how we would make it before the freezing temperatures of the pitch-black night enveloped us.

I didn't know what we'd find when we arrived. One house held memories of a past I barely knew, yet it defined every aspect of my life. The second was built by my great-great-great-grandparents. It hadn't been inhabited by humans in over eighty years. I had no memory of this house. Quint and Charlotte had each only been there once. But Pops had known my grandparents and he had been there a few times.

I felt the heat on the back of my legs and arms as the sun rose behind us. The temperature was becoming more tolerable. My fingers and toes started to warm. We each carried a small bottle of water. I tied Talin's reins to the strap of my backpack and took a sip of water, knowing it had to last all day. I untied her reins and held them again.

As I resettled the pack, a dog could be heard barking in the distance. I tensed and looked toward Jonah.

"Hold the reins tight," he said, barely above a whisper.

"One of us has to always be holding them. If I let go, you're in charge."

"Okay," I said, and doubled my grip on Talin's reins. My hands sweating more with every bark.

I walked as quietly as I could. We all did, but the barks sounded closer and closer … until Wrath was bolting through the tree line. He lunged for JP, the easiest target. East ran forward and hit Wrath hard with the butt of her gun. He shook his massive head, bared his teeth, and lunged for her. She didn't have time to react. He was too fast. In an instant East was on the ground. He tossed her from side to side like a rag doll, her arm held in his massive jaws.

Eli stood motionless. JP screamed. Jonah, in the time it took me to gasp in fear, was above his sister. He kicked Wrath hard in his side. Wrath let go of East. She clutched her arm and rolled out of the way. Jonah raised his spear. Wrath snarled and snapped at Jonah, keeping a few feet from him, stalking slowly from side to side as if trying to decide how best to kill this larger prey. Jonah watched him, his spear ready.

JP darted from behind Jonah, running to his mother. Wrath locked his eyes on the boy. The muscles in the dog's shoulders expanded as he ran hard, driven to kill. Jonah's aim was true. The life poured from Wrath's body in red pools as dark as night.

"Don't stop the horses," Quint said as he ran past me.

Though I couldn't think, I could follow the command I'd been given. I pulled on Talin's reins and picked up Fulton's discarded reins. I pulled the horses forward.

Blaise took over as head of the caravan, the rifle securely in her hands. Josh walked beside her, watching wherever she wasn't.

Nonie opened the passenger door and handed Jonah an old blanket. "Wrap the dog in this. We need the meat, and we can't have his blood leaving a trail," she said.

My stomach heaved. From behind me I heard Sara running to the far side of the road and vomiting. I turned, but I did not stop.

Jonah did as his grandmother instructed. He and Eli threw the blood-soaked blanket containing Wrath's limp body onto the top of the van. The thudding sound was followed by the startled clucking of the chickens and Sara vomiting again.

Eli used his ax as a sort of shovel to bring dirt from the side of the road over to the asphalt, in an attempt to cover the pool of blood. Jonah did what he could, using his hands to bring more dirt onto the road and his feet to spread it over the red stain.

Quint and Charlotte helped East to her feet. She was wearing a heavy coat, a sweater, and a long-sleeved T-shirt.

The dog's teeth had not pierced her skin. Though she held her arm in pain, Quint said it wasn't broken, just badly bruised. Charlotte hugged her daughter.

JP stood near his sister, crying. Charlotte picked him up. He was almost as big as her, but she carried him swiftly to the passenger door. Nonie opened the door and took him into her arms. She soothed him while he cried. Quinn seemed not to have noticed all that had happened. When JP entered the van, tears running down his face, she left her grandfather's lap and gave him a hug. Nonie held them both tightly against her. I exhaled, relieved at least those four were safe in the van.

Quint ran up and took over his spot as lead. Blaise and Josh returned to their previous posts. Jonah stayed back, watching the Jacobson property for any sign of movement. He clasped his spear, ready to defend again if necessary.

Charlotte walked beside her daughter, gun in hand. East was visibly shaken. She held her right arm bent against her body. Her left hand, holding the gun, trembled.

Sara walked with Eli. He was trying to distract her from the now red blanket on top of the van. She glanced that way every now and then and her face drained of color. He asked her a question to get her attention back to him. She took a deep breath and answered. They went on like this for a few minutes, until she finally stopped looking where Wrath lay, the blood now nearly drained from his body.

Few words had been said above a whisper. Everyone was as quiet as possible, working as quickly as possible to move us away from the spot of Wrath's death and the Jacobson property. I jumped at every noise, but Mick did not come.

Jonah returned and took Fulton's reins from me, his blood-covered spear held in his dirt-stained right hand.

We continued on. With the sun higher in the sky and the temperature increasing, I unzipped the oversized coat I wore. It was a coat Jonah had outgrown a few years back. Charlotte said they were saving it for JP. It was far too big for me, but its size made it that much warmer.

In the distance I could see the outline of Eli's car, but it looked different. As we got closer I gasped. What had once been Eli's car was now a scorched metal frame. Nothing else remained.

Charlotte started to cry softly behind us. Eli left Sara's side and put an arm around his mother's shoulders.

"It's just a car, Mom. It doesn't matter anymore, anyway," he said, holding her gun as he supported her while they walked.

"Don't you see?" Charlotte said between tears. "If this

is what he did to your car, imagine what he's going to do to our home."

My heart broke for Charlotte. I knew she was right. I knew Mick would destroy their house and then burn it to the ground. I hated him. With every step I took, I hated him more.

* * *

We reached the interstate as the sun was almost directly overhead. I hadn't noticed this the night of the light, but at the horizon there was an abandoned car heading south and, a bit closer, an abandoned truck pointed north. I wondered where the people had been going and where they were now. I felt gratitude for Jonah and East. They saved us that night. Had they not taken us with them, where would we be now? How would we have survived? The answer was, truthfully, we probably wouldn't have survived. If we had decided to leave the interstate and go east, the first house we would have come to would've been Mick's. I shook my head trying to shake out the thought.

"You okay?" Jonah asked.

I hadn't realized he'd been watching me.

"I was thinking what would've happened to us had you and East not found us that night. We were very lucky," I said.

"Like East said, luck had nothing to do with it. It was God," he said, his voice tense.

"How can you be so sure?" I asked, curiosity rising within me.

"For me it is a matter of faith, but I suppose for someone else they could look at the probability of us being a hundred yards or so behind you when the world went dark, or at least our corner of it, and you turning out to be who you are. I'm not sure how anyone could really call that a coincidence. And if it isn't just chance that brought you back to my family, then what is it?" he asked, looking at me.

"God?" I said, feeling confused.

"That's what I think," he said.

"You know I'm an atheist, right?"

"I gathered as much," he said, walking beside me.

"What do you think of that?" I asked, feeling anxious. I cared deeply what Jonah thought of me. I accepted that for many reasons we would never be together. And I knew he was going to be a priest. His world view intrigued me. It was completely different than my own and though my friends were not atheists or even agnostics, they weren't exactly devout in any faith they possessed. Jonah and his family were the first truly Christian people I had ever met.

He laughed, some of the tension leaving his voice.

"That's a funny question. What do you mean, what do I think of that?"

"I mean, does it make you not like me or think I'm going to hell or something?" I felt nervous, afraid of what his response would be. I had heard that Christians believed non-Christians were going to hell. I knew if that were the case atheists would be at the top of the list.

"First of all, atheists don't believe in hell. You are one; you should know that. Second of all, of course it doesn't make me not like you. That is your belief. I respect your belief. I don't share it, but I don't have to," he said. "Does it make you not like me or make you think I'm going to hell, knowing that I'm Catholic?" he said, a smile on his lips.

"No, but atheists are nice and they don't judge people," I said, returning the smile.

He raised an eyebrow. "Some atheists do. I've been told I'm crazy for believing in God. Naïve, ignorant, stupid. The list goes on."

"Well, that's a mean atheist, and I'm not friends with mean atheists," I said, not mentioning that my dad was one.

"So we've established we can be friends. I will go on being Catholic and you will go on being an atheist," he said, his eyes alight.

"Are you going to try and convert me or anything?" I asked.

"Do you want to be converted?"

"No," I answered.

"Then, no."

It felt good to talk to Jonah. It felt right. I knew we would never be together. But I was happy we could be friends.

* * *

We were well past the interstate. The road was now narrow, barely two lanes, and it was winding. Were we not pulling the van, we could probably cut through fields or forests to find a shorter path. But that was not an option.

I sat on the ground watching Talin and Fulton eat what few green weeds there were. JP and Quinn climbed out of the van. Unlike the rest of us they had plenty of energy. They played tag up and down the deserted road. My feet throbbed as I watched them. I wasn't sure how I would make it another mile, let alone another twenty.

Sara limped toward me and sat beside me. She took off a shoe. Her white sock was stained red.

"What happened?" I asked, shock filled my voice.

"Blisters," she said. Her hand shook as she peeled the sock from her foot.

I winced, watching her. Her foot was torn and raw, covered with open wounds.

"I think the other one is the same," she said, trying to steady her breath.

"You can't walk anymore," I said.

"What choice do I have?" she said, looking at the blood-soaked sock in her hand as if trying to summon the courage to put it back on.

"We need to get moving," Quint said, eating a piece of smoked meat as he stood.

"Sara can't walk," I said. Sara shot me a look, but I didn't care.

Quint came over and knelt beside us.

"No, she can't," he said, standing. "John Paul, you're going to walk. Jonah and Eli, help Sara to the van," Quint ordered.

"I'm okay. I can walk," she said, taking a deep breath as she moved her sock to her foot.

I pushed her hand away. My body shivering as I neared her raw flesh.

Quint turned toward his sons. "Jonah, Eli, come on, get her to the van. We have to get moving again if we have any hope of surviving the night."

They each supported her under a shoulder and carried her to the van. Nonie made room for Sara to climb between her and Pops. Sara disappeared below the dash, no doubt scrunched between the two seats and the wall of possessions.

"I want to walk too," Quinn said as Jonah tried to pick her up to put her back in the van.

"All right," Charlotte said, "but just for a little while."

Quinn ran up ahead with JP.

I groaned as I stood. I had no blisters, or at least none that had opened, but my muscles had never felt like this. I gathered the reins of both horses. Josh, Eli, Jonah, and Quint all pushed the van forward as I pulled the reins to encourage Fulton and Talin to pull with all of their might. The van began to inch forward and soon we were going a steady pace.

Everyone resumed their usual posts. Jonah returned and took Fulton's reins from me.

The road began to straighten out some and an old fence appeared on our right. It was broken in more places than it was whole and any paint that had been on it was long gone.

"This is where your property starts," Jonah said.

My heart stopped as I remembered where we were heading.

Thirteen

My steps quickened as the road switched to dirt and grass beneath my feet. The sun was gone and the temperature dropping. The deserted road would lead to my family's home: both the home I knew for a short time as a child, and the home I had never known. The home of the family who had come to this place almost two hundred years ago.

JP and Quinn had retreated to the comfort and warmth of the van hours before when the sun dropped low in the sky and the wind began to stir. JP had lasted longer than Quinn, and when he entered, Sara exited. There wasn't enough room for five of them in the van. Sara winced when her feet first touched the ground. Eli helped her hop out of the moving van. She walked slowly and gently at first, but now she kept pace with the rest of us. I wasn't sure if the pain subsided or if she was somehow walking through it.

"Just a few more miles and we should be at your old house," Jonah said.

I felt relieved and nervous. What would this place look

like? I had vague memories at best. I was now walking on ground my mom had walked on her whole life. This was the land she was raised on. This was the land she was laid to rest on. I knew she was buried here, but didn't know where. Charlotte and Quint would know, possibly even their kids. I would ask them someday, when I was ready, to show me her grave and my little brother's. I wiped a tear from my cheek.

It was dark now and there was no moon. My eyes were adjusted to the night, but still I could not see the ground beneath my feet. I put my hand on Talin's neck. I found comfort in her steady strength. I wished I had a walking stick to use as a guide, as Jonah did with his spear. Instead I lifted my feet only an inch or so off the ground, so I could still feel the weeds and loose rocks beneath them. I could hear Josh and Blaise shuffling their feet as they walked near me.

Time seemed to stand still. My body ached and the cold wind kept making me shiver. My coat now zipped tightly with the collar pulled up did what it could to protect my ears and the sides of my face. I leaned my head forward. I couldn't see, anyway; I might as well shield my face from the wind. No one spoke; we were all too exhausted. We'd stopped only one time in thirteen hours. We ate smoked meat as we trudged along and sipped the small amounts of water allotted to each of us.

The ground beneath my feet changed. The horses' footsteps rang out loudly against hard asphalt. We were on a paved road again.

"Less than a mile to go," Jonah said.

"Thank you, Jesus!" Charlotte shouted as her feet reached the asphalt. Her praise made me jump. It was the loudest noise I'd heard in hours, since the kids stopped squealing as they chased one another.

My heart raced with every step. It was getting harder and harder to breathe.

"We can stop the horses here," Quint said.

My whole body was shaking.

Jonah was close enough that I could see his face. He said, "I can take Talin from you. You can go to your house. You should be the first one in."

I felt his hands against mine as he began to slip the reins from them. My heart raced so fast I knew he must be able to hear it.

"You can do this," he said, leaning his head down, his breath warming my cheek.

"Okay," I said, barely above a whisper. I held the reins for a moment longer, forcing our hands to remain together. I took a breath, let go, and walked forward. I could see the outline of a house, my house.

I heard the jingle of keys as Quint reached the door and unlocked it.

"Careful, there's a step here," he said, opening the door. He held out his hand to help me up.

"I remember," I said, at that moment recalling my mom always waiting to hold my hand to help me in and out of the house.

When I stepped inside, my knees buckled. Quint pushed against my hand to keep me upright.

"There's a small bench to your right," he said as he stepped through the door and guided me to the bench. I sat, remembering this was where I would put my shoes on.

A moment later he was gone and Charlotte was in his place. She sat beside me. I was overwhelmed with emotion. Not having my mother in this place, where I had known her so deeply, hurt more than not having her in any other place. I missed my dad. He should be here too. The dad who had existed in this place was kind and loving. I missed that dad. I sobbed in Charlotte's arms, wishing my parents had not abandoned me.

When I calmed enough to speak, I asked, "Why did they leave me?"

"They didn't want to," she said. The tears in her eyes glowed in the firelight.

I didn't move, even after Charlotte got up to get Quinn and JP settled. The fire someone had started illuminated the small room. My eyes were drawn to it.

I watched Nonie warm some water by the fire. Quint found her a large bowl. Sara sat by the fire. Blaise helped her unwrap strips of cloth from her feet. Sara bit her lip in pain.

"Put your feet in here," Nonie said.

Sara cried out as her feet submerged.

I moved my gaze away from Sara's pain.

This was the room I had spent most of my time in. Everything was exactly how I remembered it. The red throw on the tan couch … hung just the way my mother liked it. The small kitchen table at the farthest end of the room had a cup of crayons and paper near the booster seat that was mine. Memories overwhelmed me.

* * *

"Gabriella, it's time to go. It's time for your little brother to be born." My father's voice rang with joy and nervousness. He picked up the crayons and placed them in the cup.

"But I-I draw picsure for brodder," I said.

177

"You can finish it when we get home, sweetie. There will be plenty of time later. Momma's got to get to the hospital right now," he said, leaning down to scoop me out of my chair and kiss me on the cheek.

"Get your shoes on, baby. It's time to go," my mother said as she walked toward me. Her belly was large and her face oddly swollen, even for her pregnant self.

She sat on the bench. I picked out the pair of shoes I wanted to wear. There were always several under the bench to choose from. She waited patiently as I put them on. My dad took my mom's hand.

"Thank you for making me the happiest man alive," he said as he kissed her gently on the forehead.

"You ready to go meet your baby brother?" Dad said, picking me up with one arm and carrying a suitcase with the other.

"Yesh!" I exclaimed.

* * *

Tears ran down my cheeks. I leaned forward and put my hand on the floor beneath the bench. I pulled out a purple pair of jellies. I held the plastic shoes close to me.

* * *

The cold stung where the tears had been. I could not stay in the house. I could not do it. Not now, not ever.

I still held the small shoes in my hands. I could hear Talin nearby, and I walked toward her.

"Bria? What are you doing out here?" Jonah asked, worry in his voice.

"I couldn't stay inside. It hurts too much," I said. I was honest with him to a point of embarrassment, and I didn't understand why.

"Everywhere I looked I saw the past. It was like a beautiful fairy tale that turns into a nightmare. Every beautiful memory causes me pain, unbearable pain."

Jonah held me as I cried. His arms around me felt so right. They didn't take away the pain, but they eased it.

He bent his head down. His breath warmed the back of my neck. "It's going to get easier," he said.

"I don't think so." I sniffed.

"I promise it is. As long as you don't run from the memories or the pain, it will get better."

"I can't go back in there. Not tonight. Maybe not ever, but definitely not tonight," I said, shaking my head against his chest.

He paused. "I was going to sleep in the van to be near the animals. You could stay with me if you want," he said.

"Okay," I said, wiping my eyes.

"Let me tell Mom and Dad where you are so they don't worry," he said, loosening his arms and moving his hands to my shoulders.

I nodded.

"Can I take these inside?" he asked, his hands covering my own still holding the small purple shoes.

"Yes," I whispered, releasing the shoes to him.

Fourteen

I leaned against Talin, waiting for Jonah to return. Talin and Fulton each had their wool blankets on. They were tethered to the carport. The van sat only a few feet away. The chickens remained in their cage, wrapped tightly with blankets, resting against the house.

I stared at the small window on the back door of the only real home I'd ever known. Jonah appeared, his features backlit by the fire inside. His face was thinner; he'd lost weight in the last two weeks. We all had. The effect on Jonah was what body builders worked so hard to attain: bulging muscles, no body fat.

I was always hungry. The few calories we ate every day were not enough. Quinn and JP always ate first and were allowed to eat their fill. The rest of us were allowed enough to survive. It was Charlotte and Quint who had lost the most weight. They ate last, if at all.

We had to figure out how to live in this new world. We had to find more food, which meant hunting, at least until we could plant a garden in the spring. I hoped this land, my land, would be better for us. Would allow us to eat more than barely enough to survive. Perhaps then, hunger would stop waking me from my dreams.

Jonah opened the door and walked toward me. I could see the pistol against his hip shining in the fading light of the fire.

"Bria?" he asked, his eyes adjusting to the shadows.

"I'm by Talin," I answered, petting Talin one last time before going with Jonah.

"Mom said there are blankets in the van that we should be able to find without digging through too much," he said, walking toward me.

"Okay," I said, reaching out my arm to Jonah so he could know where I was.

We walked side by side to the van. I went to the passenger side and he to the driver's side. Inside the van, I couldn't see my hand in front of my face, let alone Jonah or blankets. I knelt on the seat and felt around behind it.

"I think I found one," I said, pulling a blanket out of the pile and handing it to Jonah.

"Thanks," he said, taking it from me.

"Here's another one." I handed it to him. "There are a couple more I can get to," I said.

I pulled out two more blankets for myself. I wrapped

the blankets around me as tightly as possible.

Once I was settled and Jonah was no longer shifting in his seat, I asked, "How's Sara?"

"Not so good. Her feet are totally raw. I don't think she'll be able to walk without pain for a while," he said.

I heard him turn his head toward me.

"Tomorrow she can ride in the van, right?" I asked, facing Jonah.

"Yes, or on one of the horses. I'm not sure where the old house is on the property. I've never been there. But my guess is the van won't be able to be pulled right up to it," he said.

"How many times have you been here? To this house, I mean."

"I don't know … too many to count. My mom comes at least once a month to check on everything and clean. When I was a kid I would come with her. She cried every time for a year. Over time, she cried less and less. She always came here on your birthday or your mom's birthday, and other days that meant something—like the day of your baptism. Every few months she had me load up firewood in Dad's pickup and we'd bring it up and take back the old wood, so it wouldn't just sit here and rot. She always wanted everything perfect in case you ever came back. She always hoped you would," he said.

"I'm sorry we disappeared," I said into the darkness.

"It wasn't your fault. But it was really hard on all of us."

"On you too?" I asked, sensing the pain in his voice.

"Yeah, I cried a lot. I'm sure you don't remember, but it was a lot for all of us. My parents cried all the time. I cried all the time. Then East was born, that added to the chaos of the house, but it was good. She didn't let Mom fall apart. Mom had to take care of her and she did," he said with emotion in his voice.

"Our moms were pregnant at the same time?" I asked, not thinking about how old East was.

"Yes, Mom had East a little early, probably from the stress of losing your mom and you. She was born two months after your mom died," he said.

"That's why she's named for my mom," I said, more to myself than to Jonah.

"Yes," he said.

I could hear him nodding his head against the back of the seat.

* * *

We sat in silence. My body was exhausted, my mind racing. I wanted to sleep but couldn't. A small quarter moon rose in the sky. It was lower than the carport and shone directly into the van. The windows were fogged from our breath. The van was freezing, but warmer than the night. I felt bad for the animals. Talin and Fulton lay next to one another on the hard ground of the carport, their blankets wrapped securely around them.

I turned my head. Jonah was watching me. I'd gotten used to him looking at me. His gaze didn't bother me, though it did make me wonder why he looked at me. Jonah smiled and turned his head to look at the horses. I watched him as he gazed at them. I wished things were different. That there was some way we could be together, but I knew both of our choices made that impossible.

"What did they say when you told them I didn't want to go back inside?" I asked, wanting to hear his voice.

He turned his head toward me. "Mom and Blaise both asked if they should come talk to you. Dad stopped them and said to just give you time to get used to things. That was basically all that was said."

"Basically?" I asked.

He looked back at the horses. "Oh … well … there were no words, but East, Pops, and Josh all had stupid smiles on their faces, Eli looked worried, Sara looked a little irritated—or it could have been that she was in pain," he answered.

"What did you do?" I asked, feeling heat rise to my cheeks.

"I took Dad's pistol that he was handing me and walked out the door." He sounded irritated.

I said nothing. The irritation in his voice spoke volumes. Sometimes I thought he liked me; other times I knew he did not. This was one of those clear times when I knew he did not and I felt stupid for misinterpreting his friendship for anything more.

We sat in silence for so long I thought he'd fallen asleep.

"Bria?" he said softly.

"Yes?" I answered, turning my head toward him.

"I'm going to be a priest," he said, almost as if he were apologizing for something.

"I know," I said.

"You do?" he asked, surprised.

"East told me, the morning after Talin and Fulton were poisoned."

"Ohhh," he said, as if that explained something he hadn't understood before.

"It's good. I mean I don't get it, but it seems like if you believe in God, then it would be a good idea to work for him, right?" I said, wondering why Jonah had brought all of this up now.

"Yeah, it seems like a good idea to me too," he said, sounding relieved and confused at the same time.

"Are your parents happy about it?" I asked.

"No."

"No?" I asked, shocked by his answer.

"They don't think it's my calling," he said.

"What do you mean? It's your choice, right?"

"Yes, and they respect my choice, but they don't believe it's what God is calling me to."

Every part of his answer confused me. "What do you mean? Does God talk to you?" I asked. My eyebrows pulled together while I tried to understand what he was saying and trying not to think he was crazy for hearing an imaginary God talking to him.

"Not so much in words. More in my heart," he said, looking out at the moon.

"Oh," I said, relieved that he wasn't hallucinating on top of being delusional.

"So if it wasn't with words that God told you to be a priest, I guess that's what you mean by being called. Then, couldn't you have misinterpreted something?" I asked.

"I don't know. It felt really clear for a long time, but now … now I guess I don't know." He turned his head toward me but didn't look at me.

"The world has totally changed," I said, thinking it

must be difficult for Jonah—who believed so strongly in a God that controls things—to interpret all that had happened. It was easy for me. There was no hidden meaning or agenda. The world was as the world was, no interpretation necessary.

Jonah looked at me. "You're right. The world has totally changed."

Fifteen

I awoke to the sound of tapping. I opened my eyes to see JP's bright face staring at me through the foggy glass.

I did what I could to smile back at him. My body ached. I wanted to keep sleeping. I turned to wake Jonah. The driver's side was empty. I looked out the windshield. The family was gathering. The sun was above the horizon.

I sat up and ran my fingers through my hair. JP opened the door. The cold air made my senses jump to life. I shed my blankets, leaving them on the passenger seat, and got out of the van, shivering as I did so.

"You slept a long time," JP said, practically bouncing with the energy a new day brought him.

"I was really tired," I said, looking down at him and yawning.

JP led the way toward the rest of the family. "Why do you keep sleeping with my brother?" JP asked as we reached everyone. He was too young to know how that question sounded to my ears and everyone else's. Heat flushed through my body, as muffled laughter filled the small carport.

"I-I …"

"Because I'm the coolest," Jonah said as he walked up behind JP and gave him a playful slap to the back of his head. "Let's get going. Unless you want to go inside for any reason," Jonah said, looking at me.

I shook my head.

"Okay then, let's get Talin and Fulton hooked up," he said, walking toward the horses.

Quint helped him connect Talin as I leaned against her, petting her, wishing her good morning.

Eli and Josh lifted the chickens and placed them back on top of the van. They tied them down and threw a rope around Wrath's body covered by the frozen, blood-soaked blanket. Nonie and Quinn pushed Pops's wheelchair across the gravel drive. Charlotte supported Sara, who was limping badly, her feet bandaged inside of her shoes. I ran to her other side.

"Thanks," she said, wincing as she put an arm around me.

Charlotte and I were able to carry her to the van. She hobbled inside and sat on the floor between the two seats.

Once the horses were connected, Jonah walked over to Pops and helped him slide behind the steering wheel. The wheelchair he was using now was the kind that could easily fold up. He told me he didn't like it because it wasn't as solid as his motorized one, but that one was now useless. Eli helped Nonie into the passenger side. Quinn and JP would walk today.

We all picked up our packs and those that had weapons got them. I held Talin's reins and East held Fulton's. Quint, Eli, Jonah, and Josh got behind the van.

"1, 2, 3, push," Quint called.

East and I pulled the horses forward as the men pushed the van from its resting place. A moment later we were pulling out of the small circular drive, headed toward what would hopefully be our new home. A home I hoped held no memories for me. I looked back at my old house and quickly looked away. I was not ready to face those memories. I exhaled. Perhaps I never would be.

Jonah took the reins from East. Quint took the lead once more, this time with Charlotte at his side. They were much more relaxed today—though Quint still carried his pistol and Charlotte carried the rifle. JP and Quinn ran alongside. Quinn often stopped and waited for us to catch up before running ahead with her brother.

"Do you think we're safe here? From Mick, I mean?" I asked Jonah, quietly so no one else would hear.

He shook his head. "No. Once he figures out we killed Wrath, he'll come for us," Jonah answered, his jaw clenched as he spoke.

"So what do we do?" I asked, something close to terror rising inside me.

"We stay alert and we stay together. When he comes he might be alone or he may have some of his friends with him. We have to be ready," he said.

"How? I've never held a weapon, let alone used one. I've never been in a fight. I know how to take care of myself in a club, but not in the woods. How am I—how are we—going to be ready to protect ourselves against someone who is hunting us?" I asked, angry and terrified.

"We can train you," he said in a calm voice.

"You? No offense, Jonah, but you are studying to be a priest. Your brother is a priest. Your dad's a vet, and not the ex-military kind. How are you going to train us?"

"Just because we love God and feel called to serve him in the priesthood doesn't mean we don't know how to defend ourselves. Eli's aversion to violence is stronger than the rest of ours, so he might not be the best one to train you—though he can fight pretty well if you get him mad enough," he answered with a mischievous grin.

"None of this makes sense. Aren't Christians supposed to turn the other cheek or something? I know I've heard that," I said.

He laughed. "I'm sure you have heard that. But Jesus himself did not literally turn the other cheek when he was struck. Like most things he said, it has a deeper meaning. As Christians, we are called to love others, but we are not called to allow others to hurt us. We can defend ourselves, and we will," he said with determination.

I looked at him. He saw the questions in my eyes.

He took a deep breath. "Years ago Mick hurt our family deeply. After that my parents wanted to do all they could to protect us. They realized that short of locking us in the house—Eli was already in seminary and I was in college—they needed to teach us how to fight. More specifically, how to defend ourselves and ensure an attacker leaves far worse off than they arrived. We all learned how to protect ourselves. Not because we wanted more violence in the world, but because we wanted less. We never wanted to be victims again. So my parents, sister, brother, and I can all teach you to defend yourself. And don't underestimate Blaise. She is a really good shot. Way better than me. She could teach you how to shoot," he said, looking behind us at Blaise.

"East and your mom can fight too?" I asked, intrigued.

"East can kick my butt any day of the week. She is the best of all of us," he said.

"She always seems so scared," I said.

"She is scared. Terrified of dogs and Wrath in particular. But put her against a human and she is amazing," he said, pride evident in his voice.

I was silent. I wanted so badly to ask what Mick had done, but I knew what the answer would be. He couldn't or wouldn't tell me.

* * *

"The path is getting steeper. I don't know how much farther Talin and Fulton can pull the van," Quint said, turning to face us as he spoke.

I'd been so focused on my conversation with Jonah, I hadn't noticed the change in elevation. Pops had told me that my parents' house was a bit higher in elevation than Jonah's house, but that elevation change was so gradual it was barely noticed. This one was more drastic. Pops had said my great-great-great-grandparents had built their house on the highest point in the property. I could see now that he was right.

Not only had the elevation changed, but the ground underfoot was no longer a road, or at least not one used in the last century. The dead leaves crunched with each step we took. To my right and left there were trees in rows. The memory of crunchy sweet apples filled my mind as I spotted a lone apple rotting on the ground beneath the trunks. I scanned the trees. They were bare except for a few stubborn leaves. I wondered how many members of my family these trees had nourished. I wondered if next fall I would be here to taste the fruit of their labor. A chill ran through me as the wind caught my hair and pushed it forward toward the house, as if I were being pushed back to my origins.

The wind died down and I lifted my eyes to the horizon. Up ahead, rising from the now bare trees was the house, the home of my ancestors. Built over one hundred fifty years ago, the house was built of stone, no doubt from the property. It towered above the trees. It was not grand in appearance, but it was larger than I expected.

The reins grew taught. I turned. Talin was pulling with all of her strength, desperately trying to carry her load to me. Fulton was doing the same with Jonah. They loved us and wanted to please us. I appreciated the attempt, but wanted her to stop.

"Get some stones to put behind the tires," Jonah shouted behind us.

Eli, Josh, East, and Blaise all scattered, bringing back large stones and wedging them as tightly as possible under the tires. The largest stones were wedged behind the back wheels.

Jonah walked back to Fulton. "Unhook Talin. Once the van is emptied we will be able to get it up to the house," he said as he began unstrapping Fulton from the van.

I did as he instructed.

Eli helped Nonie out of the van. JP held her hand as she walked carefully toward the horses. She didn't need his hand, but he was trying hard to be helpful. Sara hobbled out after her and walked slowly toward the horses, wincing with every step. Quinn took her hand. Quint helped his dad to his chair and pulled him up the slope toward the rest of us.

"I don't want us splitting up," Charlotte said. "Not here."

"I agree," Quint said. "I think I can pull Dad up. Mom and Sara can ride."

"I can walk," Sara said, straightening her back.

"No, you can't. I will walk before I will let you walk," Nonie said, staring her down.

"The ground is too uneven for you to walk, Mom," Quint said.

"Then get me up on Talin," Nonie said, walking to Talin and petting her.

Jonah lifted her to the saddle, making it look effortless.

Laughing, Nonie said, "That was easier than I thought. I forgot how strong my grandson is." She slowly moved her left leg to the other side of the saddle. Quint held her steady as she got settled.

Sara stood by Fulton. Jonah put his hands under her arms and lifted her to the saddle. His movements with her were not as smooth.

"Thank you," Sara said, looking down at him.

The look in her eyes told me she still had a crush on him. As long as she did, he remained an object to her, not a person.

Jonah quickly let go once she was up. "You're welcome," he said. He was polite and kind as always, nothing more.

"Everyone grab something to carry," Charlotte said, walking toward the van.

She handed blankets to JP and Quinn. She took a box I knew contained family pictures. The rest of us grabbed what we could carry. I carried a well-worn Bible in a wooden case. The date on the front read "1696." I carried it carefully with my left hand and held the reins of both horses with my right. My backpack still rested on my back.

Jonah carried two small boxes of books, one under each arm, and his pack. We walked slowly toward the house. The ground underfoot was uneven, and I stumbled once or twice but caught myself. JP and Quinn were running ahead and each fell at least once. Quint pulled Pops backward so that he was facing me. I knew he was uncomfortable having his son take care of him in this way, but he smiled and joked as we went. I was struck, watching him, by how difficult it must be to allow others to serve you in the way he was served by those who loved him. I wondered if I would be as full of joy as he was if I were in his position. I knew I would not.

When we neared the house, my pace quickened. I felt drawn to it. I had no memories of this place. Nothing would hurt me here and it was a part of my history I had never known existed. There were several large stones scattered around the base of the house. I could see places where the stones had fallen from the house, but the holes did not appear to go all the way through to the inside. I thought it must be several layers of stones thick. Brown moss covered almost all surfaces of the house. The roof was made of some kind of thin stonelike material. It reminded me of the slate coffee table in my father's living room. The few windows were so dirty they could not be seen through.

I stared at the large wooden door. Blaise and Josh stood near me. The three of us gazed up at the large, two-story, stone structure before us.

Charlotte came and stood beside me. She held out her hand. "I knew where your mom kept this. I got it from your house last night," she said, handing me an old-fashioned key at least six inches long. She took the Bible from my arms.

Blaise and Josh took the horses' reins.

I accepted the key and put it in the lock. It took both

hands to turn the key. I looked at Blaise, who nodded reassuringly.

I turned the handle and the door clicked open. I pushed the door forward and stepped into the dim house. In front of me was a small, empty foyer with a staircase. The floors were stone, with half a century's worth of dirt on top. Moss grew here as well, creating a sort of dingy green carpet. Behind me the rest of the family entered the house, depositing their loads as they came in. Jonah and Eli helped carry Pops up the steps that led to the front door. JP held Nonie's hand as they walked in.

"Do you think it's haunted?" I heard him whisper to her.

"Of course not," she said. Then added, "We'll have your brother bless it just in case."

I walked through the small doorway to my left, not waiting for anyone else to join me. The room was dark. I went over to the drapes and pulled them open. Dust fell, creating a cloud as it drifted slowly downward. Light came through the dirt-caked windows. The room had a fireplace against the far wall. A narrow mantel above it held a small vase. In the middle of the room, facing the fireplace, was a small sofa covered with a white sheet. I pulled the sheet off, creating another cloud of dust. Beneath the sheet, the sofa was a deep red velvet with dark wood accents. Above the sofa, in the center of the ceiling, was a chandelier. My eyes followed the chain that held it as it left the ceiling and went down the side of the wall. It was hooked so the chandelier could not fall, but there was more chain hanging to the ground. It was partially hidden by a sheet-covered chair. Next to that sat a rectangular piece of furniture also covered in a sheet, and another covered chair on the other side. A worn rug extended across much of the floor. I scraped my foot over its surface, revealing a hint of green and tan beneath the dirt.

A doorway stood between the chair and the fireplace. I walked through it. As the door opened the light shone in, illuminating shelves and shelves of books. Every wall was covered with books. Books over a century old. In the middle of the ceiling was a chandelier similar to what was in the other room. A small chaise lounge sat in front of a window. I pulled the drapes open. With the sleeve of my coat I wiped part of the dirt-encrusted glass, and peered through the small, dingy pane. There were rows of trees. An orchard, no doubt. I pulled the sheet off the chaise. It was an off-white, silky fabric. Against the outer wall was another fireplace. I remembered Pops saying this house was designed before electricity. Fire was its only heat source. We would finally be warm.

I walked out the door of the library, turning the brass knob as I went. I could hear everyone coming in and out of the foyer. I wanted to be alone. I was partially hidden by the staircase and ducked quickly through the next doorway. This room had no drapes. The windows were small and sparse. There was a fireplace unlike any I had ever seen. It was large enough for me to walk around in. Inside was a large metal stove of sorts. Pots and pans hung from racks. A sink in front of the window had a small pump, like I had seen in movies. I pumped the handle. Nothing happened. In the middle of the room a small wooden table sat with four chairs around it. A door led to the backyard. I did not open it. On the other side of the room was another door. I opened it and walked through it.

I pulled the drapes open. A large table with many chairs took up most of the space. Another door led back to the foyer. I wanted to go upstairs. I opened the door and peeked into the foyer. Jonah stood alone, looking at the pile of things we had brought with us. I walked toward him, hoping to slip behind him unnoticed.

"Where've you been?" he said without turning.

I stopped. Jonah turned to face me, his eyes curious.

"I was looking around. Where is everyone else?" I asked, keeping my voice low in case others were nearby. I didn't know why I wanted to do this on my own, I just knew I did.

"Nonie, Pops, and Sara are in there," he said, pointing to the sitting room of sorts. "Everyone else went back to the van to get more things."

"Why didn't you go?" I asked.

"Dad wanted me to stay here and keep an eye on things," he said.

My gaze moved to his hip, where he wore his father's pistol. "Are we going to always be on alert?" I asked, wishing this house would bring us safety.

"No, I don't think so. But for now we are," he said. "What have you discovered so far?"

"There are a ton of books in what must have been a library, and in the kitchen there's a fireplace big enough for me to walk around in," I said.

"Books?" he asked, sounding excited.

I nodded. "An entire roomful." I wondered if Jonah liked to read. There hadn't been time in the last week, but as life became more settled, a little easier, maybe there would be time to read.

He looked toward the library.

"What about the upstairs? What's up there?" he asked, his eyes moving to the staircase behind me.

"I'm going up now to see. You can come if you'd like," I said.

"Do you want me to?" he asked, a hint of uncertainty in his voice.

"Yes," I said, careful not to make eye contact.

"Lead the way," he said, gesturing toward the stairs.

I climbed the stairs slowly, testing each one with a little weight before placing my full weight on it.

"Do you think it's safe?" I asked, when we reached the top.

"I guess we'll find out," he said, stepping in front of me.

"That's not very comforting," I said, following behind him, taking each step with caution.

"I do honesty better than I do comforting," he said as he gently placed one foot after the other.

"That's not so good if you're going to be a priest," I said, becoming more comfortable every time I put my foot down. The floor was solid; it barely even creaked.

"I disagree. Honesty is always better than a lie, even if the lie creates short-term comfort," he said, turning a doorknob and pushing the door open. There were four more closed doors off the landing.

We walked into the room. Beams of sunlight shone through the drawn, threadbare drapes, and illuminated the small room. A fireplace filled one wall and a piece of furniture spanned the other. I walked to the wall opposite the door and pulled open the drapes. The fabric disintegrated in my hands.

"These drapes must have been made from a more delicate fabric than the ones in the sitting room downstairs," he said, walking over and looking up at the fabric that remained hanging.

"The library and dining room also have solid drapes," I said, releasing the fibers of fabric from my hand. They floated gracefully to the floor, disappearing into the dust.

"Oh, I see," Jonah said, pulling a sheet from a piece of furniture. "It's a crib. This must have been a nursery. Perhaps your great-great-grandparents used some sort of fancier fabric for these drapes."

My heart stopped. The thought of a baby sleeping here brought up so many emotions, none of them good.

"Are you alright?" Jonah asked, seeing the expression on my face.

"Cribs make me uncomfortable," I said before I realized what I was saying.

"Because of your baby brother?" His voice sounded sympathetic. He placed his hand on the side of the crib, his thumb rubbing the smooth wood.

"Yes," I said, walking out to the landing.

I disagreed with Jonah. I did not think honesty was always better than a lie.

I pushed the pain down and entered the next room. I drew back the drapes and these did not crumble in my hands. There was a fireplace and a queen-size bed, and a dust-covered rug that took up half the floor. Jonah followed me, but said nothing.

He pulled the drapes open in the next room. This room was larger, with a four-poster bed with bits of fabric hanging from each post, the remnants of a canopy. I found a small writing desk with a bench seat and a dresser, all covered with sheets that created clouds of dust when I pulled them off. The wood beneath the sheets was a beautiful cherry. The furniture was so small and fragile appearing, I was afraid to touch it.

The fourth room was similar to the second room, with a fireplace and a queen-size bed, but it did not have a rug. The final room was a bathroom with a large claw-foot tub and toilet of sorts.

"I've never seen a toilet like that," Jonah said as he stood behind me and peered into the room. It had a large box mounted on the wall high above it, with a cord hanging from it.

"Do you think there was running water?" I asked. "I

saw a pump thing in the kitchen."

"I don't know. Pops and Nonie will know."

"I hope so. It would be really nice not to have to bring water in with buckets," I said.

He backed out of the room. "That would be nice," he said with a hint of exhaustion. He had carried more buckets into the house than any of us.

We went down the stairs side by side. I liked having him near me and sometimes, like now, I thought he liked being near me too.

"The house seems solid. Aside from the inches of dirt and dust, it seems in really good shape," he said as we stepped onto the main floor.

I nodded. "I feel good here. I don't know why, but I do."

"Maybe that's a good sign. Maybe we will actually have peace here," he said.

"You know I don't believe in signs," I said, looking up at him.

"Yes, but I do." He gazed down at me, his green eyes making my heart race.

Sixteen

The day passed as we took load after load into the house. My body ached. My head spun. I hadn't eaten or had anything to drink since yesterday. The sun was setting as we hooked Talin and Fulton to the empty van and pulled it up the hill. From time to time the men had to help push, but for the most part Talin and Fulton were able to pull the vehicle up the incline. Wrath's body was still in the blood-soaked blanket on top of the van. I glanced at it from time to time and quickly pulled my gaze away. The thought of Wrath brought the thought of Mick and the fear that he would come for us. That he would do to us as we did to Wrath, though his actions would not be out of self-defense but out of revenge.

We pulled the van near the barn/garage. I wasn't sure what to call it because it contained both stalls for animals and an old truck. Probably one of the first ever made. The truck looked to be in pretty good shape. It had been well covered before Josh and Blaise discovered it. The building it was in was another story. Part of it was made from the same kinds of stones of the house and those parts were standing, but other parts had been made from wood and those parts were badly weathered. The roof, too, was not made of the stone material of the house roof, but instead, of wood shingles, many of which were no longer there. Fixing the barn would be a massive undertaking, especially without power tools or cut lumber. But Pops and Nonie knew things the rest of us didn't, about how things had once been done before machines. They would know how to fix the barn.

With the setting sun came the dropping temperature. Jonah and I unharnessed Talin and Fulton. I had gotten to be good at this and could do it quickly, but tonight my fingers were stiff from the freezing wind. Jonah led Fulton away from the van, toward the back of the barn. I followed with Talin, zipping Jonah's hand-me-down coat around me as I walked. I unrolled the sleeves, allowing them to slide down and cover my hands.

Jonah stood near the stream. This was why we had come. Why we had made the two-day journey. Why Charlotte and her family had left everything. Fresh water for our animals and for us. Fulton drank the cool water, and my mouth watered. I wanted to do the same. I was so thirsty. Talin bent her head, her lips touching the water. I knelt beside her. I placed my hands in the water. It felt like needles against my skin. I didn't care. Thirst overwhelmed me. I cupped my hands, bringing water to my lips.

"Don't do it, Bria." His words were soft, his touch gentle.

"What?" I asked, as if waking from a daze.

"Don't drink the water," he said, looking down and offering me a hand to help me stand.

My hand dripping, I placed it in his. The warmth of his touch spread through my body. He pulled me up.

"I know it looks clean, but it will make you sick. Wait a little longer. Mom said she was going to boil water. I'm sure it's done by now. We just need to get Talin and Fulton taken care of and we can go in." His voice was quiet, his eyes kind.

I said nothing. I was too thirsty, too hungry, too overwhelmed by how hard it was to survive. I missed walking out of my apartment and getting a smoothie or a sandwich on my way to class. I missed having food that I paid for rather than saw killed or harvested. How was I going to survive here? At the Pages' house it didn't seem as real as it did here. Here we had stepped back in time. I knew it offered us the greatest chance at survival. I knew we had to come here, but part of me wished we hadn't. The Pages' house was comforting to me. Although none of the appliances worked it still looked normal. Here there was nothing that looked like home or the life I had known. A tear escaped down my cheek.

Tilting his body toward me, Jonah said, "It's going to be okay, Bria. We're going to be okay."

"How do you know?" I asked.

"I have faith," he said, smiling.

"How can you?"

"I just do," he said, wiping the tear from my cheek.

I leaned into his touch. I hadn't meant to, but I couldn't stop myself. His hand pressed gently against my cheek. His fingers caressed my cheekbone, moving up to touch my hair.

"We should go in," he said, closing the gap between us as he spoke.

He didn't take his hand away. He didn't want to. He wasn't just being nice; he wanted to be with me. He wanted to be close to me, to feel my skin against his. He felt something for me. Was I just the possibility of something physical? That's what it would have been for another guy, but Jonah wasn't like other guys. He was good and kind. He was pure.

I was not.

I moved from his touch.

"You're right," I said, "we should go in."

I registered the hurt in his eyes at my abrupt change. My heart sank, but I knew it was better to hurt him now than for him to find out who I really was later, when we both cared more. I would stay away from him. I would not hurt this man. I would protect him from me.

* * *

The first drops of rain fell to the ground as Jonah and I stepped into the kitchen. I was struck by the warmth of the room. A fire glowed in the large kitchen fireplace, illuminating the family who sat and stood around the room. For the first time in two days I was warm enough to take off his hand-me-down coat.

"You two look exhausted," Charlotte said.

I looked then at Jonah, for the first time since pulling away from him. His eyes were bloodshot. He looked defeated and confused. I had done that to him. My selfishness had hurt someone so good. I hated myself even more. Why did I keep causing pain? Why did I keep bringing darkness into the world?

"Just hungry and thirsty," Jonah said, striding to the sink where a bucket of water sat.

Charlotte handed him a glass and then gave me one. Jonah drank his in one gulp. I took mine and sat by the fire, next to Blaise and Sara. They had been watching me since I'd come in.

"You okay?" Blaise whispered, handing me a piece of smoked meat.

"No," I said. I was tired of pretending. The reality was, I hadn't been okay for a long time.

I wanted to leave the kitchen. I didn't want to be with the rest of the family, but I was too weak from hunger, dehydration, and blood chilling cold. So I sat and sipped my water. When that glass was empty Charlotte filled it again. She was watching me. She alternated between looking at me and looking at Jonah. What must she think? We had done nothing, not even a kiss and yet I felt so guilty. Her son who wanted to be a priest, who knew no sin, had feelings for me. A woman who had made horrible mistakes that could never be undone. A woman who would only hurt him. I glanced at Jonah. A woman who had already hurt him.

I knew almost nothing about the Catholic religion. I knew they were Christian, their priests didn't marry, and the pope was their leader. I knew there were things they were against, things they called sins, or at least that's what it said online, and I knew I had committed most of them. I wanted to cry and scream. The guilt and the pain were overwhelming. I felt dizzy.

"I'm going upstairs," I said to Blaise and Sara. "I need to sleep."

Without waiting for a response I left the room, carrying the glass of water and piece of meat. My legs felt heavy. With every step up the stairs, the weight of my body became more overwhelming.

Behind me I heard footsteps. I did not turn to see who it was. I was too tired to care.

In the room I would share with Blaise and Sara, I heard the footsteps following. A small fire glowed in the fireplace, the room's only source of light and heat. I shuffled to the hearth, wanting both.

"We need to talk," Jonah said. He closed the door.

"No, we don't," I said, turning from the fire and walking to the bed. I felt the exhaustion even more as I sat on the edge of the bed.

He placed another piece of wood on the fire and then sat on the floor a few feet from me.

"What happened out there?" he asked, his voice kind, too kind for what I deserved. "You got so angry. I'm sorry I touched your cheek. I-I lost myself for a second. It will never happen again," he said.

He thought he had done something, been too forward.

"Jonah, you … you did nothing wrong. … I liked it when you touched my cheek," I said, my voice losing its sharpness.

He exhaled. "Then what happened? Why did you get so mad?" he asked, coming to sit next to me.

My heart raced. All I wanted to do was be with him. I shook the thought from my head and slid off the bed.

"Jonah, what do you want from me?" I asked, standing by the fire.

"What do you mean?" He came toward me.

"Do you just want something physical? Do you want a one-night stand?" I asked, my voice tired.

"I would never do that." His jaw was hard, his voice calm.

"Then what do you want?" I said, crossing my arms.

He stood near me, but kept his distance. "I'm still trying to figure that out," he said, confused. "But I know I don't want you to be mad at me."

I softened my voice and my posture. "Jonah, I have no reason to be mad at you."

"Then what happened out there? I saw the anger come over you," he said, taking a step closer.

"You don't know me. You don't know my past, the choices I've made," I said.

"You were angry at yourself?" he asked.

"You are a really good guy. You deserve someone equally good. You deserve to be a priest, if that's what you want," I said, looking into his eyes and begging him to hear me.

"I don't know what I want anymore," he said, looking down at me and touching my arm lightly.

We were close enough to kiss. All I wanted to do was kiss him.

I shook my head and pulled away. "If you're thinking of not being a priest because of me, then I will make it easy for you. You and I will never happen. You deserve better," I said, turning from him. At the window, rain pushed against the dark panes.

"Bria, we all have a past. But your past only controls your future if you let it. Don't let your past control you— control us." He was nearing me, his voice strong, but his tone pleading.

I had to make him understand. I had to make him see me for who I really was. I sucked the air in as my heart raced. I said the words as quickly as I could. "I'm sorry, Jonah, but I don't feel anything for you. Yeah, you're cute, way too cute to be a priest, and it would be great to hook up, but anything more than that, I can't do. If you're okay with something casual, then we could have some fun, but otherwise you might want to try Sara. She might want something more serious."

I watched emotions wash over him: sadness, confusion, disgust. My words worked.

My heart wouldn't slow, my head spun, a layer of sweat covered my body and became like ice in the cold night air. I steadied myself on the small ledge of the window.

Jonah took a few steps backward, as if I'd shot him. He turned to go, but paused at the door. I wanted him to come back—to say he knew I didn't mean those words, that I wasn't that person. He shook his head as if having a conversation with himself, and walked out of the room.

My knees weakened and I held tightly to the window ledge for support. I heard his footsteps on the stairs. The front door opened, the rages of the storm entered the house, the door closed, the storm returning to the night.

I dragged myself onto the bed, my whole body shaking. I listened to the rain pelting the window. Tears came, and they would not stop. The wind howled. My body shook violently, as if driven by an internal storm. I thought of his pleading eyes, his words: "Bria, we all have a past. Don't let it control you—control us." I felt the pain of my choice. As if it had been lying in wait for this moment of weakness. This moment where my past finally met my present, and it could overcome me, destroy me. This pain that told me I wasn't worthy. This pain that kept Jonah and me apart.

The storm would not stop. My body convulsed in pain. My mind raced with memories. Memories I did not want. Containing events I wished with every part of my existence had never happened.

* * *

Lying on my side, I watched the rain stream down the window. The fire barely glowed, and the air around me was so cold my breath turned to mist as it escaped my lips. I heard the click of the door. Blaise and Sara entered. I did not move. Blaise placed two logs on the coals. Sara hobbled to the bed and slipped under the covers beside me. I closed my eyes and lay still. Blaise stretched out on the floor by the fire. The room warmed. I listened as first Sara's and then Blaise's breathing slowed to sleep. I opened my eyes and stared out the window that was now a mirror. I looked at my reflection. Cheeks red, eyes swollen, hair a mess and unwashed. I looked how I felt and that was a relief. I was no longer pretending.

Seventeen

I opened my eyes.

"What happened last night?" Sara asked, looking at me from the foot of the bed.

The sun was up, the fire out.

"What time is it?" I asked, rubbing my swollen eyes.

"Close to noon," she said.

"Are you just waking up?" I asked her.

She sat on the bed, staring at me. "No, we've all been up for hours. Blaise and Josh were in here watching you for a while, but they needed to help do things. It's still hard for me to walk, so I volunteered to stay here," she said.

"That wasn't necessary," I said, sitting up and feeling irritated.

"I disagree, and so do Blaise and Josh," she said, her voice calm yet serious.

I looked out the window. The rain had stopped.

Sara exhaled audibly. "Bria, what's going on with you?" she asked.

"Nothing," I mumbled.

"Please don't lie to me. You come in the kitchen looking like hell. You leave looking like you could kill someone. Jonah follows you. Then he walks out of the house into a storm, spends the night in the freezing barn. Seriously, what's going on?" She lowered her voice. "Did he hurt you?"

Anger flared. "No! He would never do that."

"That's what I thought. Then what is it?" she asked, leaning toward me.

"I don't want to talk about it," I said, sitting up.

"You are my friend and I love you, but you either tell me or I'm calling in backup," she said, not letting up.

"What do you mean, backup?" I asked.

"Everyone, everyone is concerned about you—about you two, to be exact," she said.

"You've been talking about Jonah and me?" The anger in my voice turned more noticeable than I'd intended.

"Of course. We have no TV, no movies, no Internet. You two are basically our entertainment, and God knows we need entertaining," she said, half teasing, half serious.

"What have you all said?" I asked, feeling betrayed.

"Nothing, really. There's been a lot of eyebrow raising. No one knows what's going on. Jonah isn't talking either. Though he has spent the morning with Eli. But Eli never tells anyone anything. It's probably a priest code or something," she said, shrugging.

I was glad he was confiding in Eli. Hopefully Eli could talk some sense into him. Help him see that he simply has a crush, nothing more.

"There's really nothing to say. There was a misunderstanding. We set it straight. That's that," I said, hoping she'd let it go.

I could tell by her eyes she didn't believe me.

"Have you two slept together?" she asked.

"You know we have," I said, too irritated to answer the implied question. She and I viewed sex differently. She viewed it as a goal, as a win of sorts. I did not.

"No, I mean, have you … you know," she said, intertwining her hands.

"Say the word, Sara! Sex. No, we have not had sex, nor will we ever," I said, no longer trying to hide my anger.

"He doesn't want to?" she asked, unfazed.

I leaned my head against my hand in frustration. "Sara, he deserves to be a priest or at least to be with someone good. He does not deserve to be with someone like me," I said, fighting back tears.

"Bria, that's ridiculous. He's exactly the kind of guy you do deserve," Blaise said as she and Josh walked through the open door.

"Ugh," I groaned, and laid my head back down on the century-old pillow.

Blaise sat beside me and Sara. Josh sat on the floor, looking up at us.

"As much as I hate to admit it, you and Jonah do seem to fit really well together," Sara said with a nod.

"You know if Sara is saying that, it must be true," Josh said.

"Hey!" she said.

"Sara," Blaise said, "you know you have a crush on every guy you meet—and let's be real—Jonah is amazing."

"Hey!" Josh said.

"You know what I mean. Just because I'm madly in love with you doesn't mean I can't recognize when other guys are incredible," she said, with a wink to Josh.

"Incredible? Amazing? When's the last time you described me that way?" Josh said, pretending to be hurt.

"You know I'm right," she said, glaring at her fiancé.

"Yeah, I know. I'm just giving you a hard time. That guy is pretty awesome. I have a crush on him and he's definitely not my type," he said, teasing.

I threw my pillow at him.

"What? He's a great guy. You should totally be with him," he said, throwing it back at me.

"I know he's a great guy, but that's the thing. He deserves more than me," I said, lowering my gaze to stare at my hands.

"Bria, no offense, but Trent has you messed up. He made you believe you deserved someone like him and could do no better," Sara said.

"You're wrong. Trent told me what I already knew was true. Trent and I were a good match. He was no better than me," I said, looking at Sara.

"That's putting it mildly," Blaise said, grimacing.

"He was nowhere near good enough for you," Sara said with frustration in her voice.

"You didn't know him like I did," I said, not sure why I was defending him.

Sara spoke, her voice more serious than I was used to. "Perhaps, but I knew you with him. You are better with Jonah. Even with all of the craziness around us. All the stuff with your mom and dad and brother, even with all of that. When you are with him you are okay and actually happy. That means something."

"Sara's right," Blaise said, standing. "If you choose to be miserable in life, realize that it's your choice, because Jonah is incredible and if you walk away from that, you're a fool."

"You don't understand," I said, fighting back tears. "When I say I'm not good enough for him, I'm not being melodramatic. There are things in my past you don't know about."

"Bria, we all have a past. If Jonah is half the man I think he is, your past won't matter," Josh said, touching my knee.

I wished he was right, but I knew he was wrong. Some things change us forever and forgiveness can never happen.

* * *

We spent the day cleaning and getting settled. I stayed with my friends and avoided Jonah. He must have been avoiding me just as carefully. I didn't see him. There were several times I could tell Charlotte and Nonie wanted to talk to me, but I never gave them the opportunity. I stuck to Sara and Blaise. They tolerated my presence, though when we were away from the others they told me I was being stupid and I needed to get over whatever was in my past. But they didn't know what that past was and no matter how many times they asked, I would not tell them.

The days continued in this way, with Jonah and I avoiding one another. Each of us easily filled our time with hard work and training. East took the lead in training my friends and me in combat. JP often joined in and occasionally Eli, Quint, or Charlotte, but never Jonah. We learned to punch, kick, elbow, and knee. We learned how to get away from an attacker with a knife to our throat or a gun to our head. We did push-ups and squats. Never had I worked so hard or hurt so much. None of us knew if these defenses would save us, but we all agreed we had to do whatever we could.

Jonah, Blaise, and Josh went hunting when the meat was getting low, which was fairly often, considering how many of us there were. Wrath's body had given us only one full meal, but we were thankful for that meal. Pops was right. This land had plenty of game. And Nonie and Charlotte talked often about the fresh fruit we'd have in the fall from the large orchard.

The water was plentiful. Not only did we have a stream, but it was spring fed. It originated a few miles from the house. Eli and Jonah had gone exploring one day and found that there was a house of sorts near its starting point. Pops said that was something called a spring house. The water could be diverted through the house and things like milk or cheese could be kept cool year round. The little house was designed to function like a refrigerator. If we ever had a surplus of food and weren't afraid of being attacked, we could use it as one. The horses could get someone there and back in less than an hour. But as it was, we never had a surplus of food and we were always on guard for an attack. None of us went anywhere alone, and one of us was always armed.

Quint assumed that by now several of Mick's relatives had made it out to his property. By his count, there could be as many of them as there were of us. I tried not to focus on the possibility of an attack, but it was never far from my mind. Quinn, in particular, was kept close to the house, with lots of people around her. She was never allowed to go on hunting expeditions, as JP sometimes was. She was barely allowed to go to the barn.

The horses were happy in their new home. Jonah, Quint, East, Eli, and Sara spent much of their energy building a fence to keep them from wandering too far from us. They could jump it if they wanted, but the truth was they didn't want to. They liked being near us and we liked being near them. I visited Talin often, though never when Jonah was around.

I rarely spoke to Jonah, yet I was not unkind to him. He did his best to avoid me, but he was not hateful toward me, which is how I would be to him if the situations were reversed. He was doing a tremendous amount of physical labor—cutting trees for firewood and the fence—and the result on his body was intense. His already muscular frame became even more so. I tried not to look at him. Looking at him led me to a place I knew I could never go.

We were all getting stronger. I noticed changes in my own body, which previously would only have happened with an abusive personal trainer and a near-starvation diet. Here it happened without trying. The fat melted and the muscles grew. I ate everything I possibly could. Though I was now always able to eat my fill, I rarely felt satisfied. Simple carbs, which had been so plentiful before, were now nonexistent.

Blaise, Josh, and Charlotte spoke often of the garden. Where it would be. What would be planted where. They started a compost pile not only for the horse and chicken manure, but also the bone and blood meal from the animals we ate. The skins were preserved. Nonie knew how to do that, and they would be saved until we needed the leather for shoes, clothes, blankets, or whatever else. Nothing was wasted now. Like Jonah said over a month ago, there was no more trash being added to the landfill.

The days were hard but short. We could only work when the sun was up. When it was down we had to be in. It wasn't safe or productive. We decided Mick would steal the animals before he would kill them. If they were taken we would get them back, but if only two of us were guarding them at night we knew Mick would not hesitate to kill us. As a result none of us were allowed out at night. We rotated who sat up all night guarding the house. But only those who could shoot well were in the rotation. I was never chosen.

In spite of this fear, the evenings were peaceful. If you sat right in front of the fire, the flames were bright enough to read by; otherwise, we talked or the Pages prayed. I knew now the beads were called rosaries. Eli had explained the rosary's origin to us. Sara said she thought it was a beautiful devotion to a beautiful lady. She often joined in. While I didn't join in, I found the meditative quality of the prayer relaxing and comforting. I often found myself wanting to do the sign of the cross when they finished, but I always stopped myself.

I questioned many things as the days and nights went on. I found myself believing that a God must exist. Clearly these people knew him. And I did not believe they were insane or foolish, as my father had taught me to see religious people. During the rosary or Bible readings I would look at their faces. They were so devoted. They fully believed what they were reading or praying. I saw the peacefulness in each of them, not only during prayer time, but all the time.

It was during these times, when Jonah and his family were bowed in prayer, that I watched him. Charlotte occasionally noticed my gazing at him, and I'd quickly turn away. She never said anything. Jonah never noticed.

As the days went by, the crush I'd felt for him changed. It was no longer a crush. I loved him, completely and totally. I longed to tell him. To ask him to give me a chance. To ask him to forgive me for my past actions, which I had come to see as sins. But I knew this was not fair to him. The reality was he deserved better. He deserved the best. He deserved to be a priest, to make God his spouse, as Eli had explained it to me.

The family had Mass, their church service, every morning right before sunrise. Sara began attending almost every day. Blaise and Josh also attended pretty often. I never purposely woke up to go, but I often was awake so I often went. That, too, I found beautiful, steeped in rituals I didn't understand, but they did. It was during Mass that Jonah often helped Eli, who was in charge of the whole thing. I could see him there, being a priest like his brother. I wanted to cry and rejoice at the same time. I knew it was what was best for him, and as my love for him grew so did my desire for him to be a priest. The truth was I loved him enough to give him up.

We had very few crackers left and only two bottles of wine; they were reserved for the Mass, to be used as something called the Eucharist. Eli said, "This is my body which I have given up for you." He lifted the crackers and the family bowed their heads. With the wine, he said, "This is my blood which I have given up for you." He lifted it, and again the family bowed. They then took turns eating a tiny piece of cracker and sipping a tiny bit of wine. Except for Quinn, who they said had not yet reached the age of reason when she could fully understand that this tiny bit of cracker and sip of wine were somehow turned into Jesus's body and blood.

The rest of us did not join them in the Eucharist, as they called it, though Eli said he'd be happy to teach any of us about it that wanted to learn. Sara took him up on this and he spent time explaining the Mass to her. At first I thought she did this as a way to spend time alone with Eli. I didn't think his being a priest would deter her from trying to sleep with him, but within a week I saw a change in her. I realized that in fact she was believing all of this. It was not just a ploy to get closer to Eli; it was real. She was more peaceful and less craving of attention, especially from Eli and Jonah. It was a needed change.

I was happy for her. I began to wonder if perhaps I should ask Eli to explain things to me as well, but I had just started to believe in the possibility of a God. I wasn't ready to become Catholic too.

Eighteen

The snow was coming down in sheets and had been all day. I sat on the carpet in the library, reading to Quinn. Almost everyone else was there as well. Only Blaise, Josh, and Eli were missing. It was the warmest, best-lit room in the house. I understood why my ancestors had made it the place of reading and gathering.

"What do you want for Christmas?" Quinn asked, sitting on my lap and looking at the ancient copy of *The Night Before Christmas*.

I glanced at Jonah, who sat by his mother, reading. I thought of my father. There were so many things I wanted.

While growing up, I never celebrated the birth of Jesus. My father would buy me presents for New Year's Day, but he refused to give me anything on Christmas. Now, in this Christian house, everyone was looking forward to the fast-approaching holiday. Even me.

"Hmm, I'm not sure. What do you want?" I asked, looking down at her.

"Crayons," she said.

"Crayons?" I asked, surprised by the simple clarity of her answer.

"I forgot them and everyone else forgot too," she said, looking sad.

"Oh, I'm sorry," I said, giving her a hug.

"That's okay. Santa will bring them," she said.

"Quinn, remember I said this year Santa has so many children who are in need of basic things like food, that he might not be able to give you crayons," Charlotte said from her nearby spot at the window, where she sat sewing some of JP's clothes.

"I know he will. I been good all year," Quinn said with confidence.

"We will see," Charlotte said with a hint of sadness in her voice.

"Why do you want crayons so badly?" I asked.

"'Cause I want to draw pretty pictures to put in my room," she said.

"The walls *are* a little bare," I agreed.

Pops had told us that over the years my relatives had taken paintings they liked. The result was only a few pieces still remained in the house. The walls were a dingy white; they could use some decoration or paint. We had neither.

"They are boring," she said, nodding.

"Come on, Quinn, give Bria a rest. Pick out another story and I'll read to you," East said, taking her sister's hand and lifting her off my lap.

I lay back. Reading had made me tired. Having a day inside, not cleaning, was a rarity. I lay by the fire and closed my eyes. I listened as East read to Quinn.

* * *

I opened my eyes. The sun was low in the sky. Only Charlotte remained in the room. She sat, still repairing clothes by her place at the window.

"Where is everyone?" I asked, sitting up and pushing my hair back.

Charlotte looked up and smiled. "You must have been tired. You slept through the excitement of the snow stopping and the kids clamoring to get outside and make a snowman. Everyone else went with them."

I stood and walked toward Charlotte and the window. I could see everyone playing in the snow. Even Pops occasionally scooped up a snowball and tossed it gently at Quinn and harder at JP.

"That looks like fun," I said, sitting next to Charlotte on the small couch.

"You should join them." She gave me an encouraging look.

I watched Jonah scoop snow and throw it hard at East. "That's okay," I said, glancing back at Charlotte. "What about you? Why don't you go outside?"

"I want to get these clothes repaired. John Paul has always been so hard on his clothes. Actually, all of my boys wore out knees faster than they outgrew them. But now I can't go buy more. I do have some hand-me-downs from his brothers, but not a ton, and what we have has to last," she said as she sewed a piece of homemade leather onto the ripped knees of a pair of jeans.

I wondered what it must be like to be a mother in a world as uncertain as ours.

"Bria, can I ask you something?" she said, almost reluctantly, putting the pants on her lap.

"Sure, I guess," I said, feeling nervous.

"Do you like my son?" she asked, looking me in the eyes.

"Yes, your sons are wonderful," I answered, hoping it was enough and knowing it wasn't.

"That is very kind, but I am speaking about Jonah. Do you have feelings for him?" Her gaze stayed steady.

I averted my eyes. "I … I …. Why do you ask?"

"I know it's not my place, but it's obvious that he cares deeply for you. And there are times when I see you looking at him and a moment ago you said his name in your sleep," she said.

I exhaled. My hands became wet. I rubbed them on my jeans.

I took a deep breath … deciding to be honest. "I do care for him, a great deal. But …." I paused, rubbing my hands across my thighs over and over again.

"But what?" she asked kindly.

I looked at her and bit my lip to keep the tears in. "But we can never be together."

"Few things in the world are that absolute, Bria," she said with a slight smile.

"This is," I said, with sorrow in my voice.

"I see," she said. "Just know that if you ever want to talk to me, not as Jonah's mom, but as your mom's best friend, I'm here."

"Thanks, I—"

"And also know I love you," Charlotte said. "For the person you are. Regardless of whatever happens or doesn't happen with you and Jonah. I think of you as one of my own. There is nothing you could say or do that would make me love you less. And any man, including my son, would be lucky to be loved by you. Do you understand?" she said, holding my chin in her hands and staring into my eyes.

I nodded. I wanted to doubt her words, but the force of

them made that impossible. She offered me unconditional love. All I had to do was accept it. I had never been offered such a love before.

I heard the kitchen door open and loud laughter enter the house.

She released my chin. "And now the rest of my wonderful family needs me. I know they must be hungry," she said. "I love you, Bria, and your mom loves you," she said, smoothing my hair and laying the jeans in her sewing basket by the couch.

I sucked in air, trying not to cry until she left the room. The door closed behind her as the tears slowly rolled down, dripping off my chin.

The door opened. I quickly wiped my chin on my shoulder.

"Oh, I-ah, I didn't know anyone was in here," Jonah said, stopping in his tracks when he saw me.

I sniffed. "No, it's okay. Your mom and I were just talking. You can stay. I'm going to help her get dinner together," I said, standing.

"No, you can stay. Mom sent me in here to get a dry pair of pants for JP. She said she had just finished patching a pair." He stood by the door, not moving.

"Oh, here," I said, picking up the pants. I walked to Jonah and held them out for him.

He reached out his hand. "Thanks," he said, taking them from me. "Are you okay?" He tilted his head to see my eyes.

"Yeah, just allergies or dust or something," I said, releasing the pants from my grip.

He nodded and turned to go out of the room. He stopped with his hand on the doorknob and turned to me. "Bria, I know when you're lying," he said, and then walked out of the room.

I stepped backward and fell onto the couch. He knew. He knew I lied that night ... that my horrible words had been said to keep him away and hurt him, but were not who I was.

He was staying away from me because he understood that's how it had to be, not because he hated me. Maybe someday I could tell him my secrets and maybe he would forgive me. Maybe someday he would love me as I love him. My heart was full of gratitude. Had Charlotte sent him to me on purpose? She was a smart woman. There were plenty of other people she could have sent in to grab a pair of pants. Jonah walking into the room as I was crying was not a coincidence.

* * *

A few hours later I lay on my side watching the fire burn, as Sara and Blaise slept on the bed above me. My thoughts turned to Charlotte and her family, who had given us so much. Who had saved us. I wanted to do something for them to show how much they meant to me, but there was nothing I could do. Blaise at least could hunt and had contributed to our meat supply at least once already. Josh, though smaller than Jonah, worked alongside him and was able to keep up with him at least when it came to stamina. His strength was not quite there, but no doubt it would be soon. Sara, for her part, had taken great interest in their religion. She spent as much time as she could with Eli, asking questions and learning. She too worked hard serving others. She seemed to model herself after Charlotte in that respect. But me, what did I do? I could think of nothing. Everyone else contributed in a substantial way; I did not.

What had I done today? Read to Quinn and then took a nap. A long nap that kept me from sleeping tonight. I thought of Quinn, how sweet and kind she was. At first her presence had made me uncomfortable; however, I no longer saw her as representative of *a* child but as herself. Now she made me happy and lightened my heart. I enjoyed reading to her and spending time with her. I tried to keep JP from picking on her. She would be heartbroken two days from now when Santa didn't bring her crayons. Charlotte would be heartbroken for her. I knew there was nothing I could do, but I wished there were.

Nineteen

My eyes opened to the memory of a cup filled with crayons. The gold embers of the fire glowed. The moon shone through the window. I sat up. Blaise and Sara still slept.

If I left now, I could make it to my parents' house and back before anyone had enough time to worry. Talin could get me there and back in a little over an hour if she didn't mind galloping, which she never minded for me.

I crept out of my bed on the floor. The house was silent. Jonah was on watch in the library. I hoped he was asleep. I tiptoed down the stairs, careful to avoid the few that squeaked. In the kitchen I grabbed some smoked meat and stuffed it in my pocket. I retrieved the keys to both houses. They had been in the same location since our arrival. I carefully unlocked the deadbolt and used the ancient key to lock it back. Being raised in DC I could never leave a door unlocked.

I walked to the barn, the ice-covered snow crunching softly beneath my feet, Jonah's oversized coat wrapped tightly around me. It was not a full moon, but it was not a new moon, either. There was enough light to see and the sun would be up for our return trip. Talin seemed to be waiting for me. I skillfully prepared her for our ride. Within minutes I was on her back and we were galloping away from the house, toward the house my parents had shared.

I pulled her to a stop as we left the drive of the house. I turned, thinking I saw something move in the distance. I strained my eyes but could see nothing.

I gave her a gentle squeeze and we were running again.

We made it to the house in no time. I tied her up under the carport, retrieved the key from my pocket, and fit the key in the door lock. The handle turned. I stepped back. Charlotte had locked it when we left. I know she had. My heart raced hard in my chest.

I opened the door slowly … the palm of my hand ready to drive someone's nose into their skull, like East had taught me. I waited. Nothing happened. The house was silent.

I stepped in. My breath caught. The house had been ransacked. What had remained in perfect order for almost twenty years had been destroyed sometime in the last two weeks. Anger and fear rushed through my veins.

I hurried to the kitchen table. The crayons had been scattered. I collected them in the cup and placed them in a zippered pocket in my coat. I checked the house. I didn't want to see the rest of it, though now that it no longer looked like my house it was in some way easier. I did not feel the sorrow; anger was the dominant emotion. I went into the room that would have been my brother's. Diapers had been strewn all over the room, but otherwise there did not appear to be any other damage.

I moved on to my room. It too had suffered little damage. Clothes were thrown everywhere, but nothing more. My parents' room was different. It had been destroyed. Drawers opened, contents emptied. As I entered, I stepped on a small book. I reached down. A picture of my parents fell out of it. I picked it up and opened the book to put it back in. I saw my mom's handwriting. The book was a journal—my mom's journal. I slipped it into a pocket and left the room.

The sun was starting to rise. The rising sun brought clarity. The house had been ransacked by Mick and his friends. It could have happened tonight. I walked to the fireplace and placed my hands on the ashes ... still warm. They had been here only hours before.

My mind remembered the moving shadow near the house. Mick had been there. They had been getting in position to attack.

I turned, hurrying toward the door. I heard Talin pawing at the ground and huffing. She only did that when someone approached. My heart raced. I slipped into the kitchen and grabbed a pan. I crouched down so I could not be seen from the window, and waited.

The doorknob turned. I clutched the pan, my hand sweating. The door opened. A man walked in ... tall and thin. Deathly thin. I stood behind him. I held the pan with both hands like a baseball bat. The man stood motionless, looking at the house. I pulled my arms back and brought them forward. The man turned. I saw his face. I stopped the pan inches from his nose.

"Dad!" I exclaimed, allowing the pan to fall to the floor as I stared in disbelief.

"Bria?" His eyes blinked.

We rushed to each other, holding on so tight it was hard to breathe.

My father, who had stopped crying when my mother died, sobbed like a baby in my arms. I held him as he said over and over again, "You're alive, you're alive. My God, you're alive."

My eyes moistened as I felt his starved body shake in my arms.

"How did you get here?" I asked softly.

"I walked," he said, still holding me as if afraid to let go.

"You walked? From Washington?" I asked.

He nodded.

"Did you have food or water?" I asked, feeling his spine protrude against his thin back.

"I drank snow when I could find it," he said, his speech slow.

I pulled back and looked at his haggard face, his dull eyes, moist with tears. "And food?"

He shook his head. "It's been a while."

I cried as I handed him the smoked meat from my coat pocket. He sat on the small bench by the door, slowly eating. The act of eating seemed to exhaust him. His eyelids lowered.

"When's the last time you slept?" I asked, kneeling beside him.

"A few days, since I hit the storm. I was afraid if I stopped I'd freeze to death," he said, leaning his head against the wall.

He started to fall asleep.

"Dad, I'm sorry, but we have to go. The Pages are in trouble. I have to get to them," I said, holding his hand.

"The Pages?" I saw the surprise in his deep-set eyes.

"Yes, I've been with them. The light flashed as we were approaching their exit and we met two of their kids, Jonah and East," I said, pulling my dad to his feet.

"Charlotte and Quint are okay?" he asked, following

behind me as I pulled him out of the house.

"They were, but I'm not so sure now. We have to go to them," I said as we reached Talin.

"Come on. She can carry us both."

I helped him up. He held onto my waist. We rode as fast as we could toward the house. My father rested his head on my shoulder and quickly fell asleep. I fought back the tears as I thought of all he had been through to get here.

How had he known I was here?

Twenty

I led Talin into a thicket of trees as we approached the house. The sun was up. There would be no using the cover of night.

"Dad, wake up," I said gently as I straightened my back to force him awake.

He sat up.

I slid off Talin and tied her loosely to a tree. I petted her nose and leaned my forehead against hers.

"Pray for me," I whispered to her.

My dad got down. He stretched his back.

"What's going on?" he asked. The little food and brief rest had made him more alert.

"I don't know. They've been afraid a neighbor, Mick Jacobson, would attack, and I think he has," I said, angling closer to the house, my dad following in my tracks.

"Mick? That kid is bad news," he said as we reached the edge of the tree line. We couldn't risk going any closer without being seen.

"He's not a kid anymore and he hates the Pages," I said.

"Footprints," my dad said, pointing to tracks that went from the tree line, not far from where we stood, to the house. My heart stopped at the confirmation. Someone had been here watching the house. When I left, I missed them by minutes, maybe seconds. My body shook at the thought. And now there was no sign of them. They must be in the house.

I forced myself to breathe. I had to stay calm. I had to think.

"If we get to the barn, we could get closer to the back windows without being seen," I said.

Dad nodded, and we began to follow the tree line toward the back of the barn. Once we were far enough back we ran to the barn. It should have blocked us from being seen from the house. We listened and heard only Fulton and the chickens. We looked through the cracks in the wall and saw only the animals. We slid through the door and kept to the side. The front, main barn door was wide open. I hadn't left it that way.

I looked around, but saw nothing out of the ordinary. We hugged the side, slipping into the stalls so as not to be seen from the opening. We leaned against the wall closest to the house. There were knotholes in the wood large enough to peer through.

On the snow between the house and barn lay a man. The snow near him was stained red. Jonah's spear stuck out of his chest.

"Do you know who that is?" Dad whispered.

"No," I said.

Only a month ago this sight would have made me cry out in fear. Now I felt no fear, only relief that it was not someone I loved.

Walking in front of me, Dad said, "I'm going to the window to see what's going on. I'll signal when it's safe for you to come."

I grabbed his arm. "No, I'm smaller and faster and I've eaten in the last week. I'll go. When I signal to you, try and pull the spear out when you come. We'll need a weapon." I took a breath, keeping low and steering wide of the dead man and the direct sight of the window.

In no time I was against the house. I could hear talking inside, but I could make out no words. I waited. No one came out … the voices didn't change. I crawled toward the window. When I was directly below it I took a breath and raised my head as little as needed to see in.

There were three of them. None of them faced my direction. Without turning my head, I waved my hand to signal my dad to come.

While the sight of the dead man behind me caused me

no pain, the sight I now saw made me want to jump from my hiding place and attack. If I died, I died. I did not care.

My father came up behind me and peered in. The spear, clasped in his right hand, stained the snow red beneath it.

Jonah was the only one facing the window and he looked only half conscious. He was tied, arms behind him, to a chair, his pale green shirt stained a brownish red, covered in blood that still flowed from a wound in his shoulder. His face, bloodied and swollen, hung down. Blood and saliva were dripping from his mouth. His beard was no longer brown, but a deep red.

Mick held Quint's pistol in one hand and Quinn in his other. His fingers curled tightly around her thick black hair. Tears rolled down her cheeks. Mick pointed the gun at her head. The threat of hurting her was how he controlled everyone else. The rest were seated on the floor, near the cold fire. Quint looked badly beaten, as did Josh, East, and Charlotte. Everyone's hands were tied behind them. Mick limped. The two men with him held rifles pointed at the family. JP sat behind Sara and Blaise at the back of the room. They blocked him from seeing or being seen. Pops was in his chair and Nonie sat beside him on the floor. Eli sat at the front and center of his family. His head was not lowered. He hadn't been beaten yet.

"Now what?" one of the men said, his voice muffled

through the window glass. He looked as malnourished as my father.

"What do you mean, now what? Now we take what we want, who we want," Mick said, his expression smirking, going from East to Sara to Blaise, and then settling on Quinn. "And kill the rest."

I shivered as the hatred I felt coursed through my body. I wanted to kill him, to personally kill him.

"Then what are you waiting for?" a second man, this one larger than Jonah, said.

Jonah's head lifted. His eyes were almost swollen shut. He saw me through the small slivers of eyes he had left. My heart ached. He would die if he didn't get help soon. They would all die if we didn't do something immediately. There was no reason for Mick not to start shooting the "ones he didn't want." It wasn't hard to imagine what would happen to those he took. My stomach heaved, and I swallowed hard to keep the contents down.

My dad pulled me down. "I'm going in. You stay out here," he said.

"No," I answered. "We need to draw them out. To get them to split up."

He nodded. "I'll go down to the kitchen door," he said.

"I'll try and signal to Jonah to get them outside," I said.

He nodded again, and then looked at me. "Bria, I love

you. I'm so sorry for everything. For everything I didn't do. For your whole life since your mom died—" His voice choked. "I'm sorry."

"I know. I forgive you," I said, touching his gaunt face.

He blinked the tears back and was gone, crawling toward the kitchen door. Once he passed the large chimney that jutted from the rest of the house, I turned. He could not be seen by anyone now. There were no windows between the door and the chimney.

I raised my head. Jonah was looking in my direction. Nonie and Pops had been pulled away from the rest of the family. They would be the first to die, old and of no value, in Mick's disgusting mind.

I signaled to Jonah, hoping he understood. I held up one finger and pointed toward the back door. I mouthed, "One outside, now."

I sank back into the snow and crawled as fast as I could to the kitchen door.

I heard a sickening thud and Mick scream, "What? What did you see?"

I reached my father just as the door opened and the largest of the men came barreling out. His gun rose. My father did not hesitate or flinch as the man fired directly at him. He plunged the spear into the man's abdomen. The man pulled himself off it, blood flowing down his body like a waterfall. He shot at my father again, this time hitting him in the leg. My father did not stop. He rushed forward and thrust the spear into his heart. The man fell, blood pouring from his wounds.

"You're shot," I said, rushing to my dad.

"I'll be okay. We need to get inside." He ripped the shirt off the dying man and tied its blood-soaked fibers tightly around his thigh.

I walked to the man. His eyes were open but unseeing. I inhaled and pulled the rifle from his clenched hand.

A shot rang out in the house. Without thinking I ran into the house. Another shot, followed by screaming. My father was behind me, limping as he ran. I stopped at the closed library door. My father ran in front of me, pushing it open. Jonah's head hung low. Blood poured from a second gunshot wound, this one to his chest. I looked around. Pops's head hung low in his chair. Sobbing, Nonie covered his body with hers. They were the only adults not tied up. Mick still held Quinn. The barrel of his pistol pointed at her shaking head. My father and I skidded to a stop as he grabbed her and pulled her tightly against his body.

"Drop the gun," Mick yelled at me.

Quinn looked in my eyes. I placed the gun on the ground. Suddenly Quinn's eyes changed; the fear left and determination took over. I bit my lip, unsure of what she was going to do.

She raised her foot and stomped it down hard on his foot. When his grip loosened, she turned and punched him hard in the groin. East had trained her, too.

My father lunged at Mick, pushing him to the ground.

Quinn screamed and scrambled behind East, who was now standing. With Quinn out of his grasp, everyone was jumping to their feet.

"Go back to Sara," East yelled to Quinn, who obeyed immediately.

The man who looked like an older, thinner version of Mick, fired at me. The bullet scorched my flesh as it tore open my shoulder. I lifted my left hand and felt the groove in my skin. Quint threw his entire body into a tackle that took the man to the floor. Josh and Eli were on their feet, their hands tied, but their feet were free. The man tried to rise. Josh kicked him down. Eli kicked his gun to the back of the room.

Mick picked himself up. His gun had been knocked from his hands. My father didn't move from the spot where he'd landed. East side-kicked Mick and he slammed against a bookcase.

I ran to my father. He was unconscious. I pulled him to the back of the room where he would not be trampled. I caressed his forehead. I looked at Jonah, his head hanging low, blood gushing.

"Go! We'll help your dad," Blaise said as she nodded toward Jonah.

"He saved me. He saved us," I said through tears while holding my dad's hand.

"I will take care of him," Quinn said, taking his hand in her small trembling hands.

"Thank you," I said, touching her cheek.

Charlotte ran out the side door. She returned a moment later, her hands free, carrying several knives from the kitchen. She gave one to JP, who immediately cut Blaise's hands free and then handed her the knife. Charlotte went to Jonah first. His arms loosened, he fell out of the chair. I screamed and ran to his side. Charlotte and I picked him up and laid him flat on the ground, away from the fighting. The second shot had been close to his heart. He was still alive— barely. I pushed hard on the wound nearest his heart, trying desperately to stop the blood.

Eli came to his mother, and she cut his hands free. He took the knife and freed Josh's hands.

Josh held the knife to the man's throat. "Sit down and don't move, or you will die," Josh said, his teeth clenched.

Mick was on his feet. East smiled as he came toward her, her hands still tied behind her. She easily dodged his attempt to tackle her and spun, kicking him hard in the back.

Eli ran behind her and cut the ropes that held her hands.

"I'm not the child I once was," she said, anger burning in her eyes.

"I don't know. You still look good to me," he said, his eyes moving up and down her body.

My stomach heaved. She remained calm. She waited for him to throw a punch. She skillfully blocked it with her right hand, crossed with her left, connecting hard with his jaw.

I understood now that this was what she'd trained for. What drove her to drive us and herself so hard. She wanted no more victims. For herself to never be a victim again. And now this eighteen-year-old girl was completely dominating this man, who had to have at least a hundred pounds on her.

"Get 'em, East," JP yelled from the back of the room as East connected her foot with his side. It was not a fight anymore; there was no competition.

I turned my attention back to Jonah. Quint had left the room and returned with his vet's bag. He looked at his father and then at his son.

"Take care of Jonah," Nonie said through tears.

Quint blinked back the tears and turned his attention to his son.

"Move your hands. I have to see what we're dealing with," he said to me.

I lifted my hands from Jonah's chest. They were drenched in blood. I turned my head as Quint inspected the wound.

The thin man lay on his right side with his feet pulled behind him and tied tightly to his hands. Josh stood guard.

Eli was saying prayers over his grandfather, while his grandmother cried and held her husband's hand. JP stood behind her, his hand on her shoulder.

Mick lay on the ground. Unmoving. East stood over him, confusion instead of anger dominating her face.

Quinn petted my dad's face. His eyes were open. Blaise helped him sit against the wall. Sara ran out of the room and returned with food and water. He took it from her and weakly took a small bite of meat. I exhaled. He would be okay.

Charlotte and Quint had removed Jonah's shirt. He had two tattoos on his chest. On his left a tattoo of a rosary encircled the bullet hole. On the right were the words, THE LIGHT SHINES IN THE DARKNESS, THE DARKNESS HAS NEVER PUT IT OUT. JOHN 1:5

"The bullet missed his heart, but barely. There's so much blood. It must have …" Quint pulled the flesh open with a small metal clamp. "It did. It hit the artery."

"Can you fix it?" Charlotte said, her voice shaking.

"I'm not a surgeon and this is far from an operating room. I'll do what I can. But even if I repair it, he has lost so much blood …" he said, shaking his head. "Pray." He glanced at his wife and then back at the bullet lodged in his son's chest.

"Bria, get water boiling. I'll need to sanitize instruments as I go." He took a small scalpel from his bag, poured rubbing alcohol on it, and sliced Jonah's skin.

My head started to spin, as I ran to the kitchen. I had never been good with blood. My head began to clear as I worked to start a fire in the little oven that doubled as a stove.

Pops liked hot water on cold days. He said it was the next best thing to coffee. The small tea kettle he used sat on the stove, filled with water, waiting for him.

Tears came. It was hard to breathe. So many deaths. I shook my head. I looked out the kitchen door. I could see the man my father had killed. The other man lay close to the barn. I assumed Jonah had killed him. I knew Jonah hadn't wanted to kill him. My father, too, had not wanted to kill, but he was protecting me. He nearly gave his life for me.

I looked back toward the library. But Pops. If he died, that would be the result not of self-sacrifice but of evil. Mick. The thought of his name made the hatred grow strong. He had raped East. That much was clear. It made sense why Jonah would not tell me what Mick had done to their family. He was right; it was not his to tell.

The tea kettle whistled. I grabbed a pot holder and bowl and ran back to the library.

Blaise, Eli, and East were huddled over Mick. He had not moved. A line of blood trailed from his mouth to the floor.

Josh continued to guard the fourth man.

Nonie sat on the ground next to Pops, holding his hand. His eyes were closed, his expression peaceful. She cried silent tears. JP sat next to her. Quinn sat in her lap. They lay on her, offering and receiving comfort. Sara started a fire and continued to care for my father. He looked pale, but he sat a little straighter.

Quint focused on his son, making small movements. Charlotte came up behind me with clean towels.

"The artery was just nicked. Thank God," Quint said, pulling the bullet out and laying it on a towel. "I'll try and repair it, but there's no way. I'm not skilled enough. None of the conditions are right. Nothing is sanitary enough," he said, shaking his head in frustration.

Touching his hand, Charlotte said, "Do the best you can. Ultimately it is up to God. None of us can change that."

He inhaled, nodded, and refocused.

As Quint worked, I found myself begging and pleading with someone I'd never spoken to before. I was asking God to please save Jonah. I begged repeatedly. I promised I would be good. I promised I would not be selfish and confess my love for Jonah to him or anyone. I would let Jonah be, let him be a priest or find someone worthy of his goodness. I held his hand while his father sewed. Charlotte assisted Quint when he asked. She prayed when she was not needed.

After about fifteen minutes, East and Eli carried Mick out the door. When Eli returned he and Josh carried the other man outside, still tied. Blaise held a gun and watched him closely. She would not miss. I wondered for a moment what he'd think when he saw all of his friends dead. Then I did not care.

Sara helped my father up. I noticed for the first time how dirty and torn his clothes were. Mud was caked on the left side of his body as if he had, at some point, fallen and been halfway swallowed by the earth. I could see bloodied scabs beneath holes in the knees of his pants. He had fallen more than once. He leaned on Sara. Her shoulder beneath his armpit. The bullet in his right thigh encircled by blood that had turned his tan pants a dark red. I watched as he hobbled out of the room, Sara supporting most of his weight. I thanked God that he was okay. That he had somehow known to come to this place and had survived. I looked down at Jonah. It was a miracle that my father was alive. Perhaps God would grant another one.

East and Eli returned. Eli kept his head raised, his eyes focused on his grandmother, but East kept her head lowered. I watched as she walked toward her grandparents. She looked at Jonah as she passed by and then at me. Her expression was blank. Eli knelt by Nonie and Pops.

"Nonie, may we take Pops?" he said with all the kindness of a priest … a person who I imagined saw death in a way the rest of us did not.

She nodded, tears streaming down her worn face.

East helped her grandmother to her feet. Quinn held on to East. East held her on one side, while helping to support Nonie on the other side. JP, too, helped his grandmother. The children were crying. Eli looked sad, yet peaceful, as he slowly wheeled his grandfather from the room.

Quint lifted his head and watched them go. Tears filled his eyes.

"Not now. Don't feel that now," Charlotte said turning his face to hers. "You're the only chance our son has." Her fingers leaving stains of blood on his chin. She used a torn sheet to wipe Quint's eyes.

He looked in his wife's eyes. They were strong. He

closed his eyes, inhaled deeply, exhaled and opened his eyes.

He lowered his head and began working again.

* * *

An hour later, he closed the incision.

"He needs a blood transfusion," Quint said, leaning back and sitting on the wood floor.

"What?" I whispered.

He wiped his blood drenched hands on a towel. "A blood transfusion," he repeated.

"How do we do that?" Charlotte said.

"It'll have to be direct. Eli or I could do it. We both have O negative." Quint looked at Jonah. "Actually, we'll both have to do it. He's lost so much. I don't think one of us can donate near enough. No one else in the family can donate. We'll each donate as much as we can," he said, shaking his head.

"I have O negative. I'll donate too." I said.

"You're sure you have that blood type?" Quint said.

"It's the universal donor, right?" I asked.

Quint nodded.

"I'm sure," I said.

"Thank you, Bria," Charlotte said emotion in her voice for the first time since death surrounded us.

I helped Charlotte and Quint move the couch next to Jonah. Charlotte ran to find Eli, while Quint threaded a needle into Jonah's arm and connected it to a long tube, like the kind used for an IV in the hospital. He got on the couch above Jonah and stuck a second needle into his own left arm, wincing as he fumbled to find his vein. He released a clamp at his end. Thick dark blood flowed down the tube, coming to a stop a few inches from Jonah's arm.

"Release that clamp," Quint said to me, nodding toward Jonah.

I carefully removed the clamp, fearful that it might somehow hurt him, though I knew it wouldn't. He had been shot twice, beaten, and had surgery without anesthesia all in a few hours. Removing a clamp from a tube would not hurt him. The red liquid flowed down and into his body. I exhaled … watching, hoping, praying that the blood of his father would allow him to live.

Charlotte returned a few minutes later with Eli at her side. They both sat by Jonah. She kissed his forehead. He said some prayers over Jonah. The same I had heard him say over Pops. Charlotte cried as he said the words. Quint pinched the bridge of his nose and teared up. When Eli finished his prayers, the three of them sat in silence. I sat staring at the thick liquid flowing from Quint to Jonah.

"I'm feeling a little lightheaded," Quint said, leaning

his head against the couch.

"Then stop, Dad. I'm ready. Let me give, and you can give more later if you need to," Eli said.

"Just a few more minutes. I'll be okay," Quint said, his eyes closing.

Charlotte reached up and put the clamp on Quint's end of the tube. I watched the blood continue to drain into Jonah, until the tube held only thin red lines.

Quint's eyes opened. He looked at his wife, neither saying anything.

Quint pulled the needle from his arm, bending his elbow, and held a rag in place to stop the bleeding. Eli sat on the couch. His father placed a new needle into the tube and inserted it into his right arm. He undid both clamps and blood again flowed into Jonah. Eli sat silently, holding rosary beads in his left hand. Quint lay on the floor; he had donated too much blood. He'd probably had nothing to eat or drink since yesterday.

Charlotte used a rag and leftover boiled water to clean Jonah's broken face. She caressed his blood-soaked hair. She kissed his bruised forehead. She loved her son as no one but she could.

Charlotte kept her eyes on Eli, making sure he wasn't overdoing it. After about forty-five minutes his head leaned back against the sofa.

"Quint, disconnect Eli. He's donated enough," Charlotte said.

Quint sat up and Eli lifted his head.

"I'm okay. I was just resting," Eli said.

"No, you've done enough," she said tenderly to Eli.

Quint did as she asked and disconnected Eli.

I was reluctant to let go of Jonah's hand, but knew I had to. Eli got off the couch and took his father's place lying on the floor. I moved to his place on the couch.

"Are you sure you want to do this?" Quint asked as he prepared a needle for me.

I looked at him. "Will it help Jonah?" I asked.

Quint paused and looked at Jonah's motionless body. "Yes, I believe it will," he said.

"Then I want to do it."

I winced when Quint pushed the needle through my skin, into the small vein in my left arm.

"You're a lot smaller than Eli and me and you've already lost blood from being shot, so please let me know if you are feeling lightheaded. We don't need you passing out," he said.

"Okay," I responded, watching as my blood drained into Jonah's body.

Charlotte said, "Seriously, Bria, you have to tell us if you start to feel off. You can go from talking, to unconscious very quickly."

"All right," I said, not caring about their cautions. I would give Jonah all of my blood if it would give him a chance at life.

We sat in silence, Eli snoring softly. He hadn't exactly passed out, but the blood loss had taken its toll.

I watched the blood flow into Jonah as he lay there. It was probably my imagination, but the waxy whiteness of his skin seemed to be fading … his more normal tan complexion starting to return.

My head started to feel heavy. I closed my eyes to steady the room.

Charlotte said, "Bria? Are you okay?"

I opened my eyes. "Yes, just fine," I lied.

I felt Charlotte's eyes on me even more than before. The room continued to spin, but I did not dare close my eyes. I wanted to give until they made me stop. I wanted to stay conscious as long as I could. My head bobbed. I jerked it up and it fell back down.

"Bria, we told you to tell us when you started to feel the effects." Quint was yelling as if through a tunnel.

Twenty-One

I awoke, no longer on the couch in the library. My shoulder burned. I reached to stop the pain and winced as my hand made contact with the slit the bullet had cut into my shoulder. I forgot I'd been shot. I looked around. This was once the dining room. The room was cold without a fire. Jonah's oversized coat lay on top of me. I forced myself to sit up, though I wanted to sleep. I had to find out how Jonah and my dad were.

I practically willed myself to the library. The fire burned bright. Jonah lay on a pallet near the fire ... tightly wrapped in a blanket ... his face beaten, his body limp. He didn't look alive. I stared at his chest. It rose and fell. He was breathing. I allowed my own breath to come and go once again. Charlotte sat next to him, a silver rosary in her hand. My father sat on the small couch. JP sat beside him, looking at a book. Sara and Blaise were busy trying to return the room to some sort of order. Blaise was using rags, water, and a bucket to try and remove the blood from the wood floor.

"How are you?" Dad asked, standing and limping toward me.

"Dad, sit down," I said, meeting him halfway and helping him back to the couch.

I sat beside him and hugged him tightly. He laid his head on mine and wept.

"It's okay, Dad. I'm okay," I said, holding him.

He was beyond exhausted.

"Can I show you to a room? You need to sleep," I said, pulling back and using my oversized sleeves to wipe his face.

"No, no, I'll be okay. I just love you. I was so afraid I would never see you again. I was afraid you were dead, but I knew I had to try to find you," he said, choking back more tears.

"It's okay, Dad. You found me in time. You saved me. You saved all of us," I said, looking at him with as much happiness as I could summon. I had so many questions for him, but all I could think about was Jonah and whether he would live or die.

JP jumped to his feet and stared at my father with a look of seriousness I had never seen in his eyes before.

"Why did you come here looking for her? Why did you think she would be somewhere she didn't know?"

The way he asked the question made me wonder if he

somehow knew the answer.

My father met his gaze and said, "Her mother told me."

Charlotte and I both stared and said in unison, "What?"

JP smiled and sat back down. "I knew it," he said.

I stared at him. How had he known, and how had my father?

My father held my hand and took a deep breath. "The night our country was attacked, your mom came to me in a dream. She told me to go home to our daughter. It was so real. To be honest, it scared me. I turned on the TV to distract myself. A minute or so later the show was interrupted and the announcer said we were under attack. A second later a bright light lit up my apartment. Then everything was black. I looked out the window. When I saw the White House was black, a chill ran through me," he said, shaking his head.

Sara ran out of the room and Blaise followed her. I knew hearing about DC was too much for Sara. My heart broke for her. I looked at my father's emaciated frame. A month ago he had been a strong, healthy man. Sara's mom and sister were two women alone in a city that was violent before, but now …. I shook my head to stop the thoughts.

My dad continued. "I knew everything had changed and that your mother had told me what to do. I knew somehow you would be home. I got a pack together and my road bike and left DC. Thank God I made it out of the city before the sun came up. People were already gathering outside, but the violence hadn't started yet."

He was staring at the wall as if remembering something awful. I tightened my grip and he came back to the present moment.

"What happened to your bike?" I whispered.

He squeezed my hand. "It was a long journey. Things—people are not like they were before. The cities ... the cities are very different." His eyes were growing dark, his voice barely above a whisper.

I wanted to ask him more, but the truth was I didn't want to know. I didn't want to know of the lawless violence that undoubtedly existed. I'd seen enough death, experienced enough violence. I didn't want to know what my father had been through. Not yet, anyway. It was too much. Too much for the day.

We sat in silence. Even JP seemed to recognize the severity of what my father had said, or rather, didn't say.

After several minutes, East came in and sat next to Jonah. She held his hand and stared at him for a long while.

She exhaled and looked at me. "Where did you go this morning?"

I blinked. The morning felt like a lifetime ago. "To my parents' house. I wanted to get ..." I reached into my jacket.

I had forgotten about the crayons. I unzipped the inside pocket. The plastic cup had been shattered. "These for Quinn." I stared at the pile of broken, smashed crayons in my hands.

JP got up from the other side of my father and came to me. He held out his hands. I placed the pieces in them.

"We can melt them back together. She will like them," he said, his little voice so serious.

I wondered how the day's events would affect him. He and Quinn had seen such extreme violence at such young ages. They saw their grandfather shot to death, and their brother badly beaten, shot, and … possibly killed. Had JP known what Mick had done to East? No, I was sure not. Did he understand how Mick looked at her, what he said to her? I hoped not.

"You shouldn't have gone out by yourself," Charlotte said.

"If she hadn't, we'd all be dead," East said, her tone flat.

"East, have more tact," Quint said, entering the room and going to Jonah.

Charlotte moved, giving him room to examine their son.

East replied, "After a day like today, you tell me to have more tact. That's ridiculous. You know I'm right. Her leaving is the only thing that saved us."

"How?" I asked, interrupting the bickering.

"When you left," she said, "Jonah must have followed you and realized Mick and his thugs were out there. He killed one and was not quiet about it. That's the only thing that saved us. The only thing that told us anything was going on. Otherwise, they could have come in and we wouldn't have known until it was ... too late." East's clothes were ripped and bloodstained, her body and face bruised.

"Is that what happened?" I asked, turning to Jonah. "I was so quiet, I hadn't thought he heard me."

"Of course he heard you. He notices everything you do," she said, with a look of irritation.

"We don't actually know what happened," Quint said, correcting his daughter. "Jonah was already badly beaten by the time we got to him. We fought as hard as we could, but when Mick grabbed Quinn ... we stopped." Quint shook his head.

Charlotte placed her head in her folded hands and held her rosary. The effect was that it was raised above her head.

Quint finished examining Jonah and sat by his wife. She leaned against his shoulder. He supported her.

No one spoke.

The day had been tragic. A kind, brilliant, beloved man

was dead for no reason but violence. If Jonah survived, he survived as someone who had killed, just like my father. Yes, in self-defense, but still I knew it was not what either of them had wanted. They did what they had to, to save the ones they loved.

"I'm glad you killed him," JP said, breaking the silence and looking at his sister.

"John Paul!" Quint said in a sharp tone.

East looked down at Jonah. "I didn't mean to," she said, looking up at JP.

So she too had killed. She had killed the man who had raped her. I had been raised to believe killing under any circumstance was wrong, but perhaps this was justice. I did not know.

Looking at his daughter, Quint said, "It wasn't your fault. I told you that. He was an addict. His organs were weak. Your kicks must have caused some ruptures, where in a healthy person they wouldn't have."

"His death was his doing. No one else's," Charlotte asserted, making eye contact with East.

"Whatever, he deserved to die. That's all I meant," JP said.

"John Paul, we do not decide when someone dies. No matter how evil they are. Your brother, Bria's dad, East …

they did not kill to punish. They killed to protect the lives of those they loved. Mick—" Quint's voice became too choked with hatred to continue.

"Mick killed for the sake of killing. Do you understand the difference?" Dad said, finishing Quint's thought.

"Yes, sir," JP said, watching his father.

Quint had lost his father today and possibly his son. His hand rested on Jonah's head. He petted his hair. Tears built as he gazed on his son.

We sat for a long time. My father fell asleep. I wondered how long it had been since he had slept for eight hours. East and JP left to go check on Nonie and Quinn.

I watched Jonah and his parents. Quint held Charlotte. They both cried, but both were silent now. I wanted to go to Jonah. To hold him. To lie beside him to keep him warm, but it was not my place. His parents had rights to him, not me. I sat by my father and held his hand. A hand that had once seemed so strong ... now the bones jutted against thin skin. He would not have lived much longer. He saved us today, but we also saved him.

Now we were safe. Mick was dead. He would not hunt us again. Only one of his men remained. We'd have to deal with him in some way, though I knew it wouldn't be death.

Twenty-Two

I sat beside Jonah, my foot gently resting under his arm. I didn't want to disturb him, but I had to touch him. I had to feel his skin against my own. He slept, if that's what it's called when you're in a coma. I sat between him and the fire. Its light illuminated the pages of my mom's journal. Everyone else was in bed, though I wondered how they slept.

With Pops gone, Nonie now slept with Quinn and East in the small nursery. Quinn hadn't left Nonie's side since Pops had passed. She was so young, yet very wise. She knew Nonie had lost more than any of the rest of us today. She spent her day doing what she could to help her grandmother.

Sara and Blaise slept in our room.

My father was asleep in the boys' room. He was alone.

Josh and Eli slept in the barn, guarding the prisoner. I was told his name was Heath. He was Mick's cousin. He told Eli he brought his wife and kids out to Mick's in hopes of finding food. Mick had given him a few squirrels in exchange for him fighting with Mick. Eli wanted to let him go. The rest of us said we needed time to think through options, so for now he would be kept tied up in the barn.

The bodies of his friends, our attackers, had been burned. Not out of disrespect, but out of practicality. The ground was frozen solid. There would be no digging a grave until spring. Their bodies could not be left to rot until then. As each body was laid on the fire, Eli said a prayer. All those around bowed their heads. I watched from the window. I did not bow my head, nor did I offer any sort of goodwill to their bodies or spirits or whatever they were now. They had caused immeasurable pain. Why? To revenge the life of a dog who'd tried to kill a child. I felt no pity for them, only hatred.

Pops, whom they'd killed not for survival but to cause pain, would also be cremated. For now, he lay in the sitting room he had shared with Nonie, a few candles lit around his body. Encircling him, the family had said a rosary. My father and Sara joined them. Blaise and Josh guarded Heath, though they said they would be praying for Pops.

I did not leave Jonah. I listened through the door that divided the rooms. I heard the anguish and pain in all the voices, but in my father's, most of all.

Charlotte had been with me all day, except during the rosary. Quint was in and out, but Charlotte never left. She didn't mind my being with her and Jonah. We spoke only a few words. She prayed. I watched her. Occasionally I attempted to pray, but did not know how. No one had ever taught me.

Around midnight Quint convinced Charlotte to go to bed. He said if JP awoke, he'd get scared if he didn't know where they were. I promised to watch Jonah and come get them if there was the smallest change. She squeezed my shoulder as Quint helped her out of the room.

* * *

My mother's journal was in some ways the first Christmas present I'd ever received, or ever remembered receiving. It was a gift from her to me. I hadn't told my father I had it. After all, it was addressed to me.

October 11, Feast of Our Lady of La Leche

Today, my darling child, I found out I am pregnant with you. I do not believe it possible to be happier than I am right this moment. To know that a life is growing within me. That you are growing within me. I know you will be an incredible child. How could you not be, with a father as amazing as yours. When we found out I was pregnant, he cried. You know how emotional he can be. He is so sensitive, so loving. I have no doubt you will be all those things and more. We have waited so long for you, my darling. I pray that you will be healthy and that you will grow to love God.

I love you with all of my heart! You are amazing!

Love,

Your Mom (that word feels so good to say—and write)

I closed the journal. I placed my head in my hands and cried. My mother had been so good, so pure. She loved me so much. My father had once been those things too. If she'd lived, I could have been those things. I could have grown to be loving and kind. Instead, I grew to be none of those things.

She was overjoyed and wanted me so badly. What would she think of me if she knew I had once been pregnant but did not relish in it as she had? That at sixteen I had chosen, and been encouraged to choose not to have that baby? I knew she would never be able to love me, not after that. I didn't love myself.

The guy I was dating said it was no big deal. Just abort. He didn't understand why I'd even bothered to tell him. I thought he loved me. I knew then he didn't. I felt so alone.

Isolated. Unloved. I did what he said to do. What option did I have?

I looked at the unconscious man lying beside me. I knew for him an unplanned pregnancy wasn't a choice to be made; it was a baby to be born. If he knew, he would hate me or at least see me for the evil person I was. My friends would finally understand why I was with Trent. Because I deserved far worse than he was.

My whole body shook as I cried. I realized how sorry I was. I begged for forgiveness to the only being I could, God.

I stopped crying and placed another log on the fire. I watched Jonah breathe slow and steady, as if he really was sleeping. I placed my hand gently on his chest. His heartbeat soothed me. I knew he should be dead, but watching him, I couldn't help but think maybe he would live.

I picked up the journal and flipped to the middle.

April 13, Good Friday

You learned to walk today!!!! We couldn't believe it. You pulled yourself up on the coffee table and then just let go. You made it three steps before you fell. Dad and I are so proud of you! You are such an amazing little girl!

I flipped ahead.

January 19

    It is freezing and we can't play outside. So we spent the day over at Charlotte's house. You and Jonah are inseparable. It's amazing how much he likes playing with you. You two are only 2 years apart, but when you are only 18 months, that is a lifetime of difference, literally. But he loves to play with you as much as you enjoy playing with him. You toddle after him and Eli. You fall often and Jonah waits for you or helps you up. It is so precious.

    It was a great day!

I love you!

Mommy

November 25, Thanksgiving

    I'm pregnant! How amazing is this, and to find out on Thanksgiving! What an amazing thing to be thankful for. We had been hoping and praying another baby would be joining our family and now we will have one. When he or she is born, you will have just turned 3. That is perfect timing, but then God's timing always is perfect.

I guess now I am writing to both of you. I know, little baby, that you will be just as incredible as your big sister. I am the most blessed mother ever!

I love you both!

Mommy

May 15

This pregnancy feels so different. I have this feeling that something is wrong, but my doctor says everything is fine and I just need to relax. I am trying. Bria, you help me keep my mind off things. You are so busy! It's hard to keep up with you. I wonder how I will do it with two!

Love you both,

Mommy

I put the journal down and stared at the fire. She knew so early that something was wrong. No one believed her, but she was right. How many times had I had a feeling about something that I pushed aside when I shouldn't have? The night Mick attacked, I saw him or one of them in the shadows. I should have turned around. I should have gone inside and woke people up. If I had, Jonah might have had more time. He might really just be sleeping right now instead of lying in a coma.

I shook my head and held her journal. Reading her

words was torture. Hearing about pregnancies, knowing the last one would take her life. I couldn't read about the pregnancy that killed her. I didn't have the strength.

I turned to the last entry.

August 12, Day of your brother's birth!!

I fought back the tears.

Bria,

I dreamt about you last night. It felt so real.

The contractions are coming more regularly now. Your brother will be here soon. But I didn't want to forget this.

You were standing in the backyard of my grandparents' old house. It was your wedding day. You wore my dress. Your father was there, holding your arm and crying. I knew he would cry on your wedding day. He was so thin. Eli stood in front of you, performing the ceremony. He was a priest. I was so happy to see that. I've been praying for that since his baptism.

Things were different than they are now. I don't know how. It just felt like life was not how I thought it would be for you. But you were happy. I could sense that.

I didn't stand next to you. I was off to the side. I don't understand that either—maybe that's how dreams are?

The contractions are coming so fast. Know that I love you always. Truly, my darling girl, no matter what happens in life, I love you now and forever!

Mom

I closed her journal, her love note to me and my brother. She'd written it for us so we could know we were loved. I wonder if she somehow knew she wouldn't be here for us, for me, when I got older.

I thought of the last entry. My wedding day, here in this place. The dream must have been given to her from somewhere … from God, maybe. There is no way she would've thought I would be getting married here, not when I was three.

She didn't mention the groom, but here in this place there could be only one. I looked at Jonah. The path to our wedding was not clear. The path to him living was not clear. The path, period, was not clear.

But I believed my mother, in the message she left me. I believed in hope. For the first time in my life I believed in the possibility of something more than there is. Perhaps I could become more. Perhaps I could be worthy of him somehow, someway.

I bent forward. "I love you," I whispered in his ear. I

kissed his forehead and, with my fingers, combed his hair gently away from the cuts.

I watched him for a long time. Watched him breathe. I held his hand. I wished I knew how to pray. Tears came as I asked God to let him live.

I wiped my tears and looked back at Jonah.

He did not move.

I stood and walked to his other side, not wanting to block the fire's heat. I lay beside him, touching him gently. I watched him sleeping until I could no longer hold my eyes open.

My dreams were chaotic and violent. Filled with pain and death. I watched as Mick shot Jonah, and I could do nothing to stop it. In the dream he slumped and died. I fell to my knees, sobbing. Mick turned the gun on me. My mother appeared and easily took the gun from him. He tried to fight her. She disappeared. My father appeared and fought him. Mick fell, blood trickled from his nose and ear. My father turned into East. She looked confused as she knelt beside him and felt his pulse. 'He's dead,' she said. Her face full of sorrow. I followed her gaze. Jonah lay at her feet. Blood pouring from his mouth.

Twenty-Three

"Bria, wake up!" Quinn's voice rang out through the room. "Did you see him? Did you see Santa Claus?" she asked, practically jumping on top of me.

I rubbed my eyes. Jonah lay next to me, unchanged. I sat up and spun to face Quinn. Her parents, sister, JP, and grandmother were with her.

Quint placed a log on the embers of the dying fire and began examining Jonah, his green eyes matching his son's. Charlotte knelt beside him and kissed his forehead.

"No, no, I didn't see him," I said, yawning.

"He was here! He was here!" she yelled.

"He was?" I asked, watching her excitement. Her black hair stood out in the sea of blonde and light brown hair of the rest of her family.

"Yes, see?" she said, coming toward me while opening her hand. Her dark eyes sparkled. There was a small cloth bag tied with a cloth string.

"What's inside?" I asked, knowing the answer.

"Crayons," she said in awe.

"Wow!" I said. I examined the kaleidoscope crayons, not exactly in the shape of crayons but pretty close. JP and East had done a good job turning the broken shards back into their original form.

East sat on the floor behind Quinn, delight covering her face at her sister's joy. She did so much for Quinn, always. Almost more like a mother than a sister.

The thought jarred something inside me. An image of Mick, with his jet-black hair, entered my mind. I blinked it away. I looked at Charlotte. Her eyes were bloodshot, but blue.

The breath went out of me. Quinn was not her child. Not hers and Quint's—there was no way they could have a brown-eyed child.

"Are you okay?" East asked, staring at me.

"Yes. I just felt dizzy for a second. I'm okay now," I said, looking back at Quinn, the joyous child she was. She sat beside her grandmother and JP, showing them her crayons.

Now I knew Quinn was East's daughter—and Mick's. That was why they didn't fight harder to prosecute Mick. They didn't want anyone to know the rape had resulted in a child. Mick could never know.

I shuddered thinking about what life would be like if East had made the same choice I had made. How empty this moment, and so many others, would be without Quinn. I glanced at Charlotte and Quint. They did what East couldn't. They raised her child, their grandchild, when she could not. Would my decision have been different if I had not been alone?

My father limped into the library. He stood above me, looking down at Jonah.

"Bria, would you mind taking a walk with me?" he asked, his voice unsure.

I looked back at Jonah and bit my lip.

"Go," Charlotte said, and nodded toward my father. "I will watch him."

My whole body hurt. I knew I needed to walk around. "Okay, but just for a few minutes," I said standing.

My father set the pace as we walked slowly out the kitchen door. The cold air stung my shoulder. I wondered how much worse my father's leg must feel. The bullet was still lodged in his thigh. It probably always would be. The ground had turned to mud as the snow had melted.

"Bria, I don't know where to start," he said, stopping and looking at me.

"What do you mean?"

"I want to apologize. To say I'm so sorry for everything that has happened since your mother,"—he swallowed hard—"and brother died. Walking here to you, it opened my eyes. I was alone most of the time and all I could do was think. It was the first time in eighteen years I let myself think about that day." His voice had become choked.

"I was so angry, Bria. So very angry," he said, tears filling his eyes.

"At who?" I asked.

"God," he answered.

"I thought there was no God," I said, folding my arms across my chest and feeling both pity and anger.

He placed a hand on one of my arms. "I know, and I'm sorry. I never stopped believing, but the hate and anger was so strong," he said, shaking his head.

I pulled away from him. "You lied to me. Not just about a God who may or may not exist, but about how my mother died." I paused. "Even my baby brother. You weren't there for me in any way. You were never a father," I said, my voice rising with anger.

He stepped closer. "I know, and I'm sorry. You're right to hate me. I lied about everything. I told myself it was to protect you, but I know now it was because I hadn't dealt with the pain of losing your mother and brother. It hit me so hard and it came out of nowhere. That's no excuse for leaving you, but it's why it happened," he said, his eyes pleading with me.

Had life not become what it now was, and had t. events of yesterday not been what they were, I would have held on to my anger. I would have shunned my father for as many years as he had shunned me. But we had both been shot yesterday. Pops had been killed, and Jonah ... only time would tell. Sara, Blaise, and Josh had no idea where their families were. My father had walked for a month because my dead mother told him to. I would forgive, though not forget.

"I,"—the emotion overcame me—"I just wish I'd had a dad."

He held me while I cried.

"I know. You deserved a dad who was there for you always. And I know it doesn't change things, but I promise, no matter what, to never check out again. I will be here, loving you, no matter what, until my dying day," he whispered in my ear.

He held me for a long time. It felt good to be in his arms, to feel his love.

I pulled back and wiped my eyes. Silent tears ran down his sunken face.

"Will you walk with me? I need to find Eli," he said, sniffing.

"Why?" I asked.

"I-ah, I really want to go to confession," he said, releasing me from his embrace.

I turned and started toward the barn, knowing that's where Eli was. My father followed. I wondered if confession was like I saw in the movies, where the mob boss goes to the priest and confesses all the murders he's committed. I wondered if my father would confess the killing of Mick's friend, and I wondered why.

"You know, the guy you killed deserved to die," I said as we neared the barn.

"I'm not sure anyone ever 'deserves' to die, but perhaps he did. I know if I didn't kill him, he would've killed you. I did what I had to do," he said, looking in my eyes. He turned away. "But there are many other things I've done in the last eighteen years that I'm sorry for. I want the weight of those actions, and the killing, off my shoulders. I want to be forgiven so I can start trying to forgive myself."

His words struck me. Perhaps I could be forgiven. Perhaps I could learn to forgive myself.

* * *

Eli, Josh, and Blaise sat watching the prisoner, Heath. Talin let out a loud neigh when she saw me. I went to her and gave her a hug. I petted Fulton for Jonah.

"He's going to be okay, I know he is," I whispered to Fulton. He pawed at the ground as if to agree.

"Eli, can I see you for a minute?" my father asked, his voice shaking.

"Sure." Eli stood and joined him.

My father led the way, hobbling out the back of the barn.

"How's Jonah?" Blaise asked, concern in her eyes.

"The same," I said. "But he looks a little better and his breathing's stronger," I added.

"Thank God," Heath said.

I glared at him.

"Bria! Bria!"

I heard JP's voice across the yard. I ran to him.

"What is it? What's wrong?" I asked, holding on to him.

"Come see," he said, turning and running back to the house. My heart raced with fear as I ran behind him.

We entered the library. Everyone was kneeling on the floor around Jonah.

East turned her head. Tears filled her eyes. She picked up Quinn and they left the circle, making room for me.

My heart stopped. He's dead. Tears streamed down my face. My feet felt as though they were filled with lead. The room spun. JP stood beside me. I held onto him as I sank to my knees. Jonah looked unchanged. How had he died?

His chest rose and fell.

My mind flooded and I shook my head. "He's alive?" I asked, struggling to get the words out.

"John Paul, didn't you tell her?" Quint asked, looking at his youngest.

"I wanted her to be surprised," JP said with a lightness to his voice.

Charlotte took my hand, and I looked at her, not understanding what was happening.

"He opened his eyes, Bria. Jonah opened his eyes," she said, barely able to stop the tears long enough to say the words.

End of Book One

Also by Jacqueline Brown:

Through the Ashes, Book Two of The Light Series

From the Shadows, Book Three of The Light Series

Before the Silence, A Light Series Short Story

To download your FREE copy of *Before the Silence* please visit www.Jacqueline-Brown.com

If you enjoyed *The Light,* please consider sharing your copy with a friend or leaving a review.

83567087R10178

Made in the USA
Lexington, KY
13 March 2018